The Lucky Kind

Also by Alyssa B. Sheinmel

The Beautiful Between

"This debut novel is the perfect antidote to the
'Gossip Girl'-ization of young adult literature. . . .
Endearing, realistic, and heart-wrenching."
—*New York Post*

"Sheinmel makes an impressive debut with an
absorbing tale of unlikely friendship, loss, and
family secrets. . . . The intriguing and well-defined
characterizations will keep readers riveted."
—*Publishers Weekly*

"Full of small moments and quiet realism . . .
creative and satisfying."
—*School Library Journal*

"Subdued and reflective . . . compelling."
—*The Bulletin of the Center for Children's Books*

"Touching and genuine . . . a refreshing read."
—*Justine* Magazine

"A gem of a book."
—*Austin American-Statesman*

"A memorable debut . . . emotionally moving."
—*The Knoxville News Sentinel*

"Especially refreshing . . . realistic."
—*VOYA*

alyssa b. sheinmel

Alfred A. Knopf
New York

THIS IS A BORZOI BOOK PUBLISHED BY ALFRED A. KNOPF

Visit us on the Web! www.randomhouse.com/teens

Educators and librarians, for a variety of teaching tools, visit us at
www.randomhouse.com/teachers

Library of Congress Cataloging-in-Publication Data
Sheinmel, Alyssa B.
The lucky kind / Alyssa B. Sheinmel. — 1st ed.
p. cm.
Summary: Having always felt secure within his small family, Manhattan high school junior Nick is unsettled to discover the existence of an older brother that his father put up for adoption many years ago.
ISBN 978-0-375-86785-9 (trade) — ISBN 978-0-375-96785-6 (lib. bdg.) —
ISBN 978-0-375-89866-2 (ebook)
[1. Interpersonal relations—Fiction. 2. Families—Fiction. 3. Adoption—Fiction.
4. Friendship—Fiction. 5. Coming of age—Fiction.
6. New York (N.Y.)—Fiction.] I. Title.
PZ7.S54123Lu 2011
[Fic]—dc22
2010027967

The text of this book is set in 12-point Bembo.

Printed in the United States of America
May 2011
10 9 8 7 6 5 4 3 2 1

First Edition

This book is for
Joel E. Sheinmel

Phone Calls and
Other Life-Altering Events

It's 7:42 on a Tuesday when the phone rings. I only notice the time because I'm watching *Wheel of Fortune,* which is so boring that I think I might be better entertained if I turned off the TV and stared at the blank screen. I wonder when Vanna White began looking like somebody's mom. I distinctly remember thinking she was hot when I was younger. My parents are out and I'm sunk into the living room sofa, but the phone is within my arm's reach. I grab the remote and hit the mute button.

"Hello?"

"Eh-hem."

"Hello?"

"Is Sheffman Brandt in?"

It takes me a second to realize he's talking about my dad. Sheffman is his real first name, but no one calls him that. He usually goes by Robert or Rob or Bobby, for his middle name. Sheffman is his mother's maiden name. It must be a telemarketer or someone who got his name off a list.

"No, I'm sorry, he's not home. Can I take a message?"

There's silence on the other end. I think I hear the man say "Umm," like he's really thinking about whether or not to leave a message.

"Hello?" I say, mildly irritated.

"No. I'm sorry. No. Sorry. No, thank you." His voice sounds more certain that "No" is the right answer each time he says it. Then he hangs up, so I do, too. I'm asleep before my parents get home.

In the morning, the sound of my mother and Pilot coming back from their walk wakes me up. Pilot is our dog, but my parents act like he's my little brother.

My father is sitting in the living room at his computer. His desk is in the back of the room, behind the sofa, so that he can watch TV while he works.

"Morning, Nicky," he says, looking up from his cereal. Even though he's fifty years old, my dad has a big sweet tooth; he puts three or four spoonfuls of sugar into his Grape-Nuts every morning. Mom says he's going to get adult-onset diabetes. Dad works from home half the time, and he's sitting in his pajama

bottoms with his cereal, so it doesn't look like he's going in today. Before I was born, he started a company called Fetch Capital, and my mother quit her job to help him run it.

"Hey, Dad." My hair is still wet from the shower, and my
shirt is clinging to my chest because I was still wet when I put it
on. But it's only September, school's only just started, and it's still
hot out. It'll feel good once I get outside.

My mother and Pilot are on the couch, watching the five-day
forecast, which is pretty much my mother's favorite show.

"Stevie coming over this morning?" she asks as I walk toward the kitchen.

I shake my head. "I'll meet him downstairs." Stevie and I
have been walking to school together since we were ten.

"His parents were at the fund-raiser last night. They won the
big prize in the silent auction."

"What they win?" I ask as I pour myself cereal.

"Some trip. They always bid on the trips, those two."

Stevie's parents love to travel. When we were little, Stevie
slept over every time his parents left town.

"Bring a sweater to school with you, Nick," Mom says, kissing my head before she leaves the room. "I know you think it's
still summer, but it's getting cold already and your hair is still
wet." I roll my eyes at Dad but he says, "Sweater, Nicky," like he
agrees with Mom that I'm not old enough to know whether
I'm hot or cold.

Girls in School Uniforms

"**W**hy the fuck is everyone in such a hurry to get into that building?" Stevie asks. We're standing on the corner across the street from school, leaning against the windows of the pizza place. Stevie hates school this year. His parents are making him see a tutor after school because colleges pay such close attention to junior year on your transcripts. It wouldn't be so bad if Stevie didn't already get straight As. They seem to think, since he never studies, that something must be wrong. But Stevie's just that smart. You'd hate him if he weren't so cool about it. Sometimes when we have two choices for an essay, he'll write both of them, choose the one he likes better, and give me the other one to hand in.

I'm pretty sure that Francis is the only coed high school in New York with school uniforms. Boys have to wear shirts and ties, and right now Stevie and I are sweating under our long sleeves. Whoever came up with this outfit was not thinking about the weather in Manhattan, which stays hot through September and gets hot again in May, so that the boys have to sweat out two months every year.

But not the girls. The girls wear gray kilts and button-downs, although they call them blouses, and they always roll their kilts at the waist to make them shorter. Sometimes they wear boxers underneath their kilts, and the skirts are rolled so short that you can see the boxers peeking out at the hems.

Eden Reiss is walking toward Stevie and me, and her kilt is just above her knees; she never rolls her skirt to make it shorter. Her button-down is loose enough that the buttons don't pull at her chest, but you can see the polka dots on her bra underneath her white shirt.

"Check out Eden's bra," Stevie whispers.

"Yeah, I see it." I don't exactly need it pointed out to me, and Stevie knows it. But I'm trying not to look because she'll see me staring. Eden Reiss has been at Francis since kindergarten, too, just like Stevie and me. Just her name is enough to make her cool, like her parents wanted something biblical, but rather than settle on Eve they went straight to the heart of the matter by naming her Eden.

"Praise Jesus for girls in school uniforms," Stevie says.

"You're Jewish."

"So are you. But I gotta thank someone."

"Well, thank Theodore Francis for being so uptight that when he started this school, he made the kids wear them."

" 'Praise Theodore' don't have the same ring to it."

"Let's go in already."

"Yeah, all right."

Tribeca

Most of the kids at Francis live uptown, mostly on the Upper West Side, but the Upper East, too. Eden Reiss lives in Tribeca, which is all the way downtown. She's the only person in our class who lives there. And Tribeca is my excuse to talk to Eden Reiss today. Her walk to the subway is kind of in the direction of my building, so all I have to do is fall into step with her and ask her for Tribeca restaurant recommendations for my parents' anniversary, which is next month. It's flimsy, but it's the best I can do. I barely spoke to her once last year and it's a new year and so it's going to be different. We're juniors now, which means there's only four more semesters left to get this girl. Someone's going to get her attention, and damned if I'm not going to at least try for it to be me.

I'm standing outside the building after school is over, feeling like a total jackass because I'm waiting for Eden. Stevie flashed me a thumbs-up before he left for tutoring, even though I hadn't even told him what I was planning. Crap, this is pathetic. She might have plans after school. What if she's with her girlfriends, or with Rob Mosely, who lives in the West Village and sometimes takes the subway with her? This is never going to work.

But then there she is, on her own, chewing gum, pulling her hair back with one hand and getting her MetroCard out with the other. Girls can do so much at once.

I wait until she gets started on her walk, and then fall in behind her, trying to be casual.

"Hey, Eden."

She turns back, blinking. "Hey, Nick."

"You walking to the subway?"

"Yeah."

"Me too—I mean, I'm walking home, but it's this way." Christ, I sound rehearsed.

"Oh." Eden keeps right on walking.

"How long does it take you to get home? Once you're on the train?"

She shrugs. "About twenty minutes, I guess."

"You must get a head start on reading." I don't think I could sound more like a dork at this point.

She wrinkles her nose. "Nah. I like to people watch. Have you ever noticed how we always try to fill our time with reading, or listening to music, or whatever? What's wrong with just staring into space, or at the other people? You see interesting things."

"I'll bet."

Eden nods, but she doesn't say anything else, and for, like, five steps we walk in silence. She hasn't once smiled at me.

"So, you live in Tribeca, right?"

"Yeah." She knows I know that.

"How come your parents chose Francis? It's so far away."

"My mother went to Francis."

"Really?"

"Why would I lie about that?" she says, not meanly, and not rhetorically, either. I think she may want me to answer. But I move on.

"Anyway, it's my parents' anniversary in a few weeks, and they like to go someplace new every year. There are so many good restaurants down there—any suggestions?" I'm doing everything wrong, but I don't know how to do it any better.

Eden shrugs. "Do they eat down there a lot? 'Cause I can't think of anyplace new—but there are some great places that have been there forever. Do they want something romantic?"

"I guess. My dad always makes the plan, but I said I'd help him think of something."

"Try Scalini Fedeli."

"Scalini Fedeli, got it." I know the name, because we've eaten there. But I'm not going to tell Eden that.

"Thanks," I say.

"Sure," she says, and turns onto the block where the subway

entrance is. It's out of my way, but I turn with her. She'll disappear soon, and I haven't made any kind of progress at all.

But then something happens, right at the subway entrance: Eden stops walking, and turns to face me. "I have to run." She sounds apologetic.

"Yeah, me too," I say, even though I don't have anywhere I need to be.

"One of these days I'll have to drag you downtown," she says, and she, just barely, smiles. I can see her teeth peeking out from under her plump upper lip. She looks so fresh that I think her mouth would taste like apples.

"How come?" I ask, feeling stupid.

"Show you around the neighborhood, I guess."

"Right." I don't think I've smiled this entire exchange, so I start to, to let her know that I'm friendly and that I'm enjoying talking to her, and then I stop, because I should be so cool that I don't need to smile. But then that's worse, because now this half smile of mine is hanging in the air between us.

Mercifully, Eden says, "Right."

"See you tomorrow."

"Tomorrow," she says, and hops down the stairs to the subway. When she bounces, I can just barely see the bottom of her underwear: plain gray cotton. Not polka-dotted to match her bra.

$\sim$

"Dude, she practically invited you to her bed," Stevie says later. Stevie is very optimistic about Eden Reiss. I'm sitting on my bed, a highlighter in hand. Stevie's phone call interrupted my attempt at our history homework.

"I wouldn't say that. She said 'the neighborhood.' "

"Well, that's world-class innuendo."

"Jesus, Stevie, not everything is innuendo."

"It is if you look for it." I can hear Stevie grinning.

"Hang on a sec, someone's on the other line."

"Okay, but come on back, 'cause we gotta get you into the Garden of Eden."

"How long you been waiting to say that?"

"Not as long as you've been waiting to do it, man."

I click over. "Hello?"

"Hello? Excuse me, is Mr. Brandt at home?"

I recognize the hesitant voice immediately. "Is this the same guy who called last night?"

"What?"

"Are you trying to sell us something? 'Cause we're on the do-not-call list."

"No, I'd just like to talk to Mr. Brandt."

I roll my eyes. "Hang on a sec." I click back to Stevie. "I'll call you from my cell phone. It's for my dad." Stevie and I may be the last two guys in New York who still call each other on their landlines; we've been friends since long before either of us had a cell phone. Other than my own, his home phone number was the first one I ever memorized—and I'm pretty sure that his house was the first place I ever called all by myself.

I click back to the other line. "One second," I say, and then walk into the living room and hand the phone to my dad, who's watching baseball from his desk. "Bring it back to my room when you're done."

"Who is it?"

"I don't know."

"Thanks, kid."

"I'm not your secretary," I say, but I'm smiling.

"Hello, this is Rob Brandt," he says, and for some reason, I don't walk away immediately, back to my room, to my cell phone, to call Stevie and discuss Eden, or at least to work on our homework together. I'm kind of curious who this guy is.

But my father surprises me. "Oh, hello," he says. "Yes, I usually go by my middle name," he explains, and then he's silent. "Can you hang on one second?" Poor guy's been on hold three times already tonight. Guess he's not a telemarketer.

"Nicky, do me a favor." My father hands me the phone, carefully, like it's made of glass. "I'm going to go into the bedroom. Will you hang up when I pick up, please?"

"Sure." He's acting like he's asking me to do the impossible, and this is not a big deal. The phone from my room gets fuzzy in my parents' bedroom. We do this all the time.

"Okay. Thank you," he says, breathless. I can't tell if he's nervous or excited. "Just hang up, that's all."

"I think I can handle it, Dad." He seems to cringe when I call him "Dad." Or maybe I just imagined that.

Before I hang up, I hear my father ask the guy to repeat his name. It's Sam Roth.

Stolen Bicycles

I can't imagine that my father would be in any kind of trouble with that Sam Roth guy. My father is a remarkably nice man. People always like him. He's part of why Stevie practically lives here. He always wants to watch the ball game, but he'll totally turn it off and play video games with us. And he's good, too.

My dad grew up in Ohio, in this very small town called Troy, so small that I always think it must have been a shock to his system the first time he saw New York. We go there a couple of times a year to visit his parents; we land in Columbus, where his brother now lives, and then we rent a car and drive to Troy. The only hotel in Troy is a Days Inn where the sheets always feel dirty. But we stay there, two or three long weekends a year. On the drive from the airport, as the scenery goes from city to suburb to country, I count how many billboards there are advertising Jesus. Maybe that's why I'm the only Jewish kid I know who says "Jesus Christ" when I'm surprised, or pissed off, or have screwed myself royally. Other than Stevie, that is, but he probably got it from me.

When we're in Troy, we go to church. It's a small community church, and the four families who've been going there more than one hundred years have honorary ownership over each of the four stained-glass windows. Every year we take a picture in front of the Brandt window. Once, standing in the white church, under the window, gritting my teeth for the picture, I leaned in and asked my dad—trying not to break my smile—whether his parents knew I'd been raised Jewish. Mom's Jewish, their wedding was even Jewish, with a rabbi and the seven blessings and the stomping of the glass at the end. They must know. But Dad just smiled and shushed me.

Apparently, Troy isn't as nice as it was when my dad was growing up. My grandparents like to take us to the mall, where we eat at a diner that my father says used to be his favorite restaurant. My grandparents don't seem to notice that things aren't as new as they used to be. My dad tells me that he worries about his parents wandering around that mall without him, oblivious to the fact that it's maybe not a place for elderly people to wander around.

It was at this mall that I found out my father was brave—but a quiet kind of brave, so that until then I hadn't even been aware of it. I was nine years old, and we were at the mall alone together, running errands for my grandparents. It's an outdoor mall, rows and rows of stores with sidewalks in between, kids racing by on Rollerblades and bikes and skateboards. I've always been jealous of kids who are good on skateboards because I have terrible balance. When we were little, Stevie had a skateboard and spent hours in Central Park watching me fall off it.

My father and I were coming out of the video store, having rented a couple of movies, and my father told me to wait, go back inside, just wait a second until he came and got me. I knew what he'd seen, because I'd seen it, too, but I guessed he just wanted me to stay inside until it was over. There were two boys, maybe fourteen or so, cutting the chain locks on some mountain bikes resting against a parking meter. My father walked toward them—and these were not skinny kids; they looked scary, at least in my nine-year-old opinion. But my dad walked straight to them, with his glasses and the corduroy patches on the elbows of his jacket, and he talked them out of stealing the bikes.

I know that because I recognized the look on his face when he talked to those boys. It was the same look he got when he was explaining something to me. He actually reasoned with them. I still wonder if those boys waited until we walked away and then came back to take the bikes, but I don't think they did. I think they were actually convinced by whatever my father said. My dad: so reasonably insistent, so calm.

So when he got off the phone that Wednesday night, my dad didn't shout for me or for my mother. After I hung up the phone, I went back to my room and called Stevie, then finished my history reading, and I only knew my dad's phone conversation was over because I saw him, out of the corner of my eye through my open bedroom door, walking down the hallway toward the living room. I heard Pilot trotting toward him, but my father must have not wanted to play with him, because the dog came into my room, rubber ball in his mouth, begging to play fetch. A few minutes later I saw both my parents on their way down the hall, and when they got to their bedroom, they closed the door behind them.

So now I have no idea what's going on, but I know it has to do with that guy on the other line.

History

Mr. Barsky is staring at me, like he's expecting something, some words, to come out of my mouth. Stevie's sitting next to me, and he nudges me with his elbow. I must be pretty far in outer space, because my arm hurts where his elbow hit, like maybe it's not the first time he's done that in the last few seconds.

"Nick Brandt," Mr. Barsky says, "would you care to join us?"

"Umm, yeah."

"And where are we?" Mr. Barsky's making fun of me now. He's a nice teacher, but he thinks it's incredibly rude when kids daydream in class. I can hear the other kids shifting in their seats.

"Umm ..." I try to remember what I read in last night's history assignment, something clever, something to make Mr. Barsky laugh so he won't be pissed at me for being rude, but my mind is a blank.

"Henry the Eighth's court, sir."

"Well, then you should know it's a treacherous place in which to piss off the king." Mr. Barsky's lips begin to curl. He's gonna laugh soon.

"Yes, sir."

"All right, then. Anyone else know why we should care so much about Henry the Eighth's marriage to Anne Boleyn?"

"Because of its contributions to the Reformation" comes a voice from behind my head, a voice that's kind of scratchy like maybe the talker smoked too many cigarettes last night, or didn't get enough sleep. It's Eden's voice.

"Excellent, Miss Reiss."

Today Eden's bra is blue. I saw it when she walked into the classroom, just the strap, peeking up by her neck. I wonder if she's hot, wearing that long-sleeved button-down. This classroom isn't air-conditioned, but she doesn't have her sleeves rolled up like the rest of us. She always seems somehow more crisp than anyone else. There's a softness around her breasts, and at her hips and her belly, but somehow, she's . . . sharp.

<hr />

Later, when we've finished dinner and my mom is reading in the living room, my dad comes into my room looking exhausted.

"Hey there, Buddy," he says, rubbing his eyes. I'm sitting on my bed, over the covers, doing my Algebra II homework.

"Hey, Buddy," I say back. Buddy is a nickname from when I was little. I decided a while back that I would stop saying it or answering to it, but tonight I've forgotten. I lean back against my pillows.

"This has been a long friggin' week, you know." He sits down at the foot of my bed. My mom says my dad used to curse a lot. Not like the angry kind of cursing—like I said, he rarely gets loud and angry. But just kind of peppering his sentences with "fuck" and "balls" and "sonuvabitch." When they had me, he tried to tone it down, apparently. The result is that he uses words like "friggin'," which, frankly, I think sounds worse than "fucking."

"It has?"

He looks up at me, like he's just realized that he knows something that I don't; like he forgot that I don't know whatever it is that's making his week long.

Maybe Sam Roth is trying to extort money from him. Like, Sam just looked him up, made up some dirt about him, some invented secret from his Ohio past that no one in New York knows about, and he's threatening to tell my dad's fund's investors if my dad doesn't fork over some money.

I'll cut to the chase. We can figure it out. I can help him.

"Who's Sam Roth?" I say quickly, before I can change my mind.

My dad blinks; he starts for a second, like maybe he's going to get up off the bed, maybe he's going to get my mom, maybe he can't stay sitting down. The bed actually bounces a little as he lifts his weight off of it.

"How do you know who that is?"

"I don't, Dad; that's why I just asked you. In fact, it's exactly what I just asked you."

"Right, but—where did you hear that name?"

"He's the guy who called last night. I heard him say his name. I think he called Tuesday, too. Someone called asking for you."

My dad nods. "Yes, that must have been Sam. He told me he'd tried the house before."

"He didn't even know your name. He asked for Sheffman Brandt."

"That is my name," my dad says, leaning back on the bed. I'd had him momentarily flustered, but he's composed himself now. Now that he knows how I know Sam Roth's name.

"Yeah, but no one who knows you calls you that."

"True."

He doesn't volunteer any more information, and it's not like him not to answer a question directly. I'm sure Sam Roth is trying to screw with my dad, and I want to tell him he can tell me; whatever this Sam Roth is doing to him, I'll help him figure it out.

"So, who is he?" I say, trying to make it sound casual. I try to turn it into a joke. "What's he got on you?"

My dad smiles slowly, like I've just said something right, something a little closer to the truth than he thought I could.

"Oh, that," he says. "Just some . . ."—he exhales, puffing out his lips—"just a little bit of history there, I guess."

"He from Ohio?"

He shakes his head. "Only kind of."

"How can someone be kind of from a place? That doesn't make any sense."

"It makes sense here." He smiles. "Kind of."

He sounds tired, but I won't let up.

"Kind of?"

"Yup," he says, like case closed. But he doesn't get up. He sits there, looking at me. More like watching me. I feel bad for him; he looks pretty wiped. Whatever this guy is doing to him, it must be pretty bad. Just for now, I'll change the subject.

"Speaking of history, I thought Mr. Barsky was going to eat me alive today."

"Yeah?"

"Yeah. I totally spaced in class." Because of Sam Roth, I want to add. And maybe because of Eden Reiss, too.

"Well, careful with that, Buddy. Don't want to get a reputation with the teachers. Maybe you should do some extra credit or something to make up for it."

"Jesus Christ, Dad, one space-out in the decade I've been at Francis," I say, irritated. "I don't think my reputation is destroyed just yet."

"Yeah," he says, getting up, patting me on the shoulder, "not yet."

And as he leaves the room, I think, Yeah, not yet.

The Weekend

Well, my dad may have been having a long friggin' week, but it's Sunday morning and I've been having a long friggin' weekend. Mostly because if she didn't think I was an idiot before, Eden Reiss most definitely thinks I am now.

"Jesus Christ, man," Stevie says when he calls me, "you're acting like it's the end of the motherfucking world or something. It wasn't that bad."

"Wasn't that bad?" I say, burrowing under my covers, bringing the phone with me. "Are you an idiot? Name anything worse I could have done."

"Oh, come on. Chin up," he says, and it's then that his voice

cracks and he can't hold his laughter in anymore. "If only you'd
kept your chin up last night. 'Cause you were damn sure looking
down when you threw up all over Eden Reiss's shoes."

I didn't throw up on Eden's shoes. Not even that close to
them. But close enough. She was at Simon Natherton's party,
too. She was hanging out on the roof, too. She was smoking
a cigarette and holding it lightly between her fingers, like she
didn't even care that it was there. So that was definitely close
enough.

"Jesus Christ, Stevie, don't make it any worse than it was."

"Oh, come on, it's not so bad. It's just the natural order of
things. You're a healthy American teenage boy. Only right that
you drink yourself sick."

"You didn't," I mumble.

"Can't go by me, kid. I'm mature beyond my years."

"Simon threw up, too, goddammit."

"Yeah, but he just had the good sense to do it on the street
outside the house. Not on the roof in front of everyone."

At least, it's raining today. At least, Simon's parents are out of
town until Wednesday, and at least, it's not like the housekeeper
would be able to tell that it was my throw-up.

Jesus, that's nasty. I know his housekeeper; when we were
little, we used to eat the cookies she baked after school. I should
send her something.

My head hurts. My headache travels from my left temple to
my right eye. After Stevie hangs up, wishing me a happy hangover, I lie in bed staring at the ceiling. I close one eye, then the
other, back and forth, focusing on a spot in the paint, watching

the way it moves back and forth as I look at it with one eye at a time. Then I realize that this winking process of mine is making the headache much worse and I don't know why I started doing it in the first place, so I stop and roll over to hug the pillow but I can't fall back asleep because I have to go to the bathroom too badly.

Eden barely looked at me all night; just my luck she waited until I got sick to get close to me. I only went up to the roof because I knew she'd be there. Simon wouldn't let anyone smoke in the house, and Eden always smokes at parties. I've never seen her smoke any other time. She was wearing a white tank top with jeans, and she stood out because every other girl was wearing black.

It was warm last night and Eden was sweaty. It's almost like she compartmentalizes her bodily functions the way she does her smoking: at school, dry and crisp; at parties, smoky and sweaty. I watched when she brought a cigarette to her mouth and could see the sweat that had formed on her upper lip. And when I saw that, I was glad I was across the roof from her, because I really do think that had I been closer, I wouldn't have been able to stop my hand from reaching out, my thumb from brushing the sweat away, my tongue from licking it off my finger.

And I'll bet her smoky party sweat would have tasted like honey.

I literally (and pathetically) stumble out of my bed. It's noon, and I'm just getting up, and I'm only up because Stevie called. And I'm pretty sure he only called because he wanted to make that "chin up" joke. Friggin' asshole.

"Look who's up," my dad says to me, bright and cheerful as I continue to stumble, now into the living room, where he's sitting on the couch.

"What's going on?" I ask.

"Watching the pregame. Reds are playing the Mets at one."

"Go, Cincy," I say pathetically. Dad grew up rooting for the Reds in Ohio, so I root for them, too.

"What did you do last night? You didn't get home until after two."

"How'd you know that?" A while back I convinced my parents that a cell phone was actually more restrictive than a curfew when it came to keeping tabs on me.

"Your mother wouldn't go to sleep till she heard you come in. So she kept me awake while she waited."

"You guys don't have to do that."

"She can't help it. You're her baby."

"Yeah, but I'm not *a* baby."

"She just sleeps better once she hears your door click shut," Dad says, shrugging. "Anyway, what did you do last night?"

I pause before answering. I wonder whether he and Mom would be more pissed that I was drinking or that I was doing it perched atop a roof.

"Where's Mom?" I ask finally.

"Walking Pilot."

"Well," I say, "Simon Natherton had a party."

Dad snorts at me. "I think Simon Natherton had a keg."

"That, too," I sigh, too distracted about Eden to even bother trying to cover up.

"You know," he says, stretching his arms out behind him like he does when he's making fun of me, "when I was your age we used to imagine the sophistication of the kids from New York City. Surely they weren't climbing onto rooftops, hovering around kegs like the kids from Troy, Ohio."

"How'd you know we were on the roof?"

Dad grins at me.

"Boys will be boys."

"There were girls there, too," I say, cringing at the memory, lowering myself onto the couch beside him. Why did we start inviting girls to parties, anyway? Whose brilliant idea was it to so increase our chances of humiliation? My chances in particular.

Dad sniffs. "What's that smell?" he says accusingly. I should have showered before coming out here.

"Sorry, Dad."

"You reek of cigarette smoke." He's really strict when it comes to smoking.

"It was a party."

"I don't care if it was a meeting of Winston-Salem."

"I'm sorry."

"Don't apologize to me, apologize to your lungs."

I look down at my chest. "Sorry, Lungs," I say.

"You're not funny, Nicholas," Dad says, but I can tell he's at least mildly amused by me.

The phone rings. Dad jumps as though the phone has startled him, then looks at his watch, like he'd been expecting a call at some particular time and he has to make sure this is it, this is that call at that time. He begins to get up, off the couch, as the phone rings for its second time. Then he looks back at me, remembering that I'm here, remembering that I will probably notice it if he rushes into the other room to take this call, that I will wonder what call he could possibly need to take out of my earshot on a Sunday afternoon.

And so he stands there. Not even quite standing, really, since he never fully got up from the couch. He's kind of crouching. The phone rings a third time, and I can tell he's worried he'll miss the call.

I want to just get up and go back to my room, save him the trouble. That would be the nicest thing I could do, but then I remember all the effort it took me to get here in the first place. Besides, I'd like to let him know that I know what he's thinking.

"It's all right, Dad," I say. "Take Sam Roth's call in your room."

He looks startled, but then the phone rings a fourth time, and he seems to realize that discussing this with me will have to wait, because if he lets it go much longer, he'll miss that call. From my spot on the couch, I hear him say "Hello," but then I hear his door latch shut, and then I don't hear anything.

I'm getting kind of pissed at Sam Roth. Who the hell does he think he is, taking up all this space, taking up my whole house, taking my dad into the other room to be with him?

It's the bottom of the fifth when my dad comes out. To tell you the truth, I've mostly been sleeping; it's only because of the baseball game that I know how much time has passed. I woke up for a second when my mother and Pilot came home, but my mother only went into her room—my parents' room—for a second, then she turned around and came back in here and settled herself with her laptop on the dining room table.

"Been on the phone all this time?" I ask when Dad finally emerges. He sits down on the couch and asks me for the score. I tell him and then he says, "No," in answer to my question.

"What've you been doing?" I say it accusingly, like he's the teenager caught doing something wrong. Smoking up in his room. Watching porn. Sneaking out.

He shoots a look across the room at Mom, who's looking at us over the top of her computer screen. She doesn't say anything, but Dad seems to be waiting for her.

"Dad, you won't even look at me," I say softly. I can't remember my dad ever not looking at me. Okay, once, when we were visiting his family and I was three and wrestling with my cousin Sandy, who was also three, and I kicked her between her legs and she started bleeding down there, and all the grown-ups started freaking out, and my father had to explain to me what had happened.

But that was just that he was embarrassed. Also, I think he was trying not to laugh.

"Maybe we should go to brunch," he says finally.

"What?"

"I think maybe we should all go to brunch. Aren't you hungry?"

"No, Dad, I've got a hangover the size of Texas. I'm not particularly hungry."

"You've got a hangover?" my mother cuts in, and at once

my dad and I both turn to her, because this is the first thing she's said. I find it somewhat ridiculous that my hangover is the thing she's chosen to comment on.

Mom looks at me hard when she sees the incredulous look at my face. "No matter what else, Nicky, I'm still your mother, and we'll talk about your drinking later."

I'm too distracted by the first half of what she's said to worry about the second half.

"What do you mean 'still'? 'Still' implies that there was a before and an after and that something happened in between, and so some things are now different and some things are 'still' the same."

Now I turn back to face Dad, looking at him hard. "Tell me when this switch happened that made Mom be 'still' the mom."

"We've educated him too well," Mom says, eyeing Dad. "I told you he'd figure something out." She shoots Dad a look, like "I told you so."

I'm getting more and more irritated. Whatever this is, it's something they've discussed telling me about; something they've apparently disagreed about telling me about. And she's acting like she's proud or something; she just knew her little boy would catch on.

"Jesus Christ, Mom, this isn't cute." I know I shouldn't be so smarmy; I should probably appreciate that she's the one who actually believed I'd catch on to whatever the hell this is.

"Okay, that's enough," Dad says finally, standing up and beginning to pace the room. "That's enough. I know it is. And I knew it would happen, I just . . . it's been so many years since I put my name out there, I'd begun to think . . . But still, I'd hoped that this would happen." He stops pacing now, and faces me. "I just never thought about telling you, I was so worried about what I'd say to him, and that's not fair to you. That's not fair to you. It's just that he came first." Dad laughs then. "He *literally* came first."

"Dad," I say, standing up to face him, an inch or two taller than him for about six months now, "what the hell are you talking about?"

"You sure you don't want to go to brunch first?"

"Pretty darn sure."

"When I was your age—for crying out loud, I wasn't your age—when I was twenty-one, my girlfriend's name was Sarah." He stops. "I think we should sit down." And he walks to the table, where Mom is sitting, and sits down in his chair next to her, and I sit down in mine across from them. The same seats we've always sat in, except on holidays when we have guests, who don't know whose seats are whose. Mom snaps her laptop shut and pushes it away from us.

"My girlfriend's name was Sarah," he says again. "She was my first girlfriend, all through high school, and when I went away to college, she still lived in Troy, so I'd see her when I came home from school, for holidays and things. And my senior year I had to come home in the middle of the semester, during my midterms in the spring, and I had to meet a lawyer in the hospital, and I had to sign the papers."

"What papers?"

"Papers, you know, the papers you have to sign for that."

"For what?"

"For a baby."

"Wait, what are you talking about?" I slouch more so that my shoulders curl over the table, so that I'm closer to my parents sitting across from me, like maybe if I get closer I'll understand better.

"Sarah was pregnant. And then we gave the baby up for adoption."

"Oh." Now I lean back again, feeling ridiculously like I've been swaying back and forth in my chair throughout this conversation. And then a strange sentence weasels its way into my head: *I am not my father's firstborn.*

"Oh," I repeat. Troy is like a whole other world compared to New York, so maybe my dad was this whole other person there—someone with a past, someone who kept secrets.

"I think . . ." Now Dad hunches over the table, leaning toward me. "I think you have to remember that it was a long time ago, and it was a small town." He sounds like he's defending what a big deal he's made of it. Does he think that I'm quiet because I'm thinking *just adoption*? Is there a disappointed look on my face, like I thought it was going to be something more, something bigger? If I look disappointed, that isn't why.

"It was a small town and . . ." He pauses, and keeps leaning forward, like he's trying to get closer to me, but I'm still leaning back against my chair and away from him. I think he's literally biting his tongue, trying to keep himself from saying anything. "Goddammit, in any town, it's a big deal."

"Okay, I believe you. In any town." I lean forward again so

that he knows I'm not blowing him off. "You've been sneaking around the house like there was this big dark secret, and I can't remember you ever having had a secret. I thought maybe Sam Roth was some guy trying to extort money from you."

I laugh, even Mom laughs. But Dad doesn't. He just says, "No, nothing like that," and he gets up from the table, and when his back is turned, I notice my mother shaking out her hand. I see that her fingers are white, like no blood had been getting to them, and I realize that for the last five minutes, none had, because my father, under the table, had been holding her hand so tightly.

I'm not sure what I'm supposed to do now. Am I supposed to go to my room? I guess he thinks my response was too small. Well, sorry, I don't know the proper response to finding out your father made stupid mistakes when he was younger. Things like that don't happen here. Not to anyone I know, not to anyone I go to school with. Maybe they weren't allowed to have sex ed at the public high school in Troy where Dad went. We all have sex ed, we all know we're supposed to use condoms, and any of the girls I know—I think they would all know what to do, early on. I almost asked why Sarah didn't do that, but then I thought that I had no idea what the abortion laws were in Ohio now, let alone—I do the math—twenty-nine years ago. And now that I think about it, I guess it wouldn't be a very nice thing to say, given that Sam Roth is now a living, breathing twenty-nine-year-old person.

"Did he grow up in Troy, too?" I ask, finally, to my dad's back.

"Hmm?" he says, turning around, looking down at me.

"Where did he grow up?"

"In Texas."

"Texas?"

"Yeah, we knew that when we signed the papers. That it was a family in Texas."

"Did you know they were Jewish?"

"What?"

"The name Sam Roth." I say it carefully now, allowing the name to hold weight when before it was hollow. "It sounds Jewish."

"No, we didn't know. Actually, I haven't asked him. He might be Jewish."

"You didn't think that when you heard that name?"

Dad shakes his head. Sometimes Mom and I forget that he's not Jewish, so he doesn't think of things like that. I'm sure it was one of the first things Mom thought. I bet she wonders if he was raised religiously. I wasn't.

"I've never been to Texas."

"Me either," Dad says, "not even on a business trip."

I try to think of something that I know about Texas, something that would help explain Sam Roth.

"Is he a Republican?" I say, and finally, Dad laughs.

"You know," he says, "I've been thinking about that for almost thirty years. I'm too scared to ask him."

Counting the Steps

Making Dad laugh seemed like the right time to make my exit, so I said I had homework. But I'm in my room now and I haven't even made the pretense of picking up a book. I haven't sat down on the bed or the floor or at my computer. No, I'm standing in the middle of my room looking at the floor, and then at the ceiling, and then out the window, and then at my bed, and at the pile of books beside it, calculating just how many steps it will take me to get from the center of my room to the bed (I figure five), and then how much effort it would take to reach my arm out to lift a book from the top of a pile, and then how heavy it would feel while I brought it down onto my lap, and then how far I would have to lean back to turn on the lamp on my nightstand, and then how long it would take me to fix my pillows so that I could sit up while I read. But wait, I'd need a pencil to underline and make notes while I read, and my pencils are on my desk, next to my computer, clear on the other side of the room. So if I'd done that, if I'd made all that effort to get to my bed, get my book, turn on my light, and adjust my pillows, I would have had to get up, walk a good seven or eight steps to my desk (wait, how big is my room, anyway?), pick out the right pen or pencil, and then go all the way back to the bed, pick up the book again, adjust the pillows again, and it would have been a ridiculous amount of effort to expend before I could even begin to do my homework.

I think I'm better off standing right here instead. And I try to come up with something that I can do from right here, the center of the room, a place I've begun to think of as my spot, like actors who have spots they have to hit on a set or onstage. If they're not in the right spot, then whole scenes can be ruined. Enormous efforts are made that surround their being in their spot—lighting arrangements, camera arrangements—to say nothing of the spots of the other actors with whom they're performing. One actor blows his spot and then all those other details would need to be adjusted.

And so I think, I really do think, that I should stay in my spot right now.

My cell phone is on my dresser, and that's only an arm's length away. I can reach my phone without leaving my spot. I grab it, careful, very careful not to drop it, because if I did, surely the battery would pop out and slide along the hardwood floor, and then I'd be shit out of luck, because I'd never be able to retrieve it without leaving my spot, and I'm sure as hell not leaving my spot right now.

I hold it in my hands for a minute, begin scrolling through my contacts. I can't call Stevie, even though his number was probably the last one I'd called so I'd just have to hit send to redial him, minimal effort for sure. But I can't call Stevie because I'd tell him about my dad, and I get the feeling that my dad doesn't want me to tell Stevie about this. I can't think of anything I've ever not told Stevie, but I can't think of ever having had a secret before. Only little things like sneaking out at night or the first time I smoked pot or got drunk, which of course I told Stevie, and eventually probably even told my dad about, too.

But I don't want to tell Stevie about Sam Roth, because first I'd have to admit how I was a big baby who was jealous that some stranger's phone calls were taking my dad away from me, and then I'd have to admit that I came up with that ridiculous extortion theory, and then I'd have to tell the truth, and then I'd have to talk about how pissed I am, and I just don't feel like explaining anything right now.

But who else is there, besides Stevie, to call? And I have to call someone. Otherwise, I'm just some creep who's psychologically glued to his spot, holding a cell phone and pressing the buttons like he doesn't know which ones do which things.

I call Eden. Her number's been in my phone for months. I got it from someone else—how pathetic is that—but I call Eden, who maybe won't pick up when she doesn't recognize my number, but I call Eden, because it's not like I can make a bigger ass out of myself than I did last night, right? I mean, it would be rude not to call her and say sorry about your shoes; did I get your shoes?

"Hello?"

I don't say anything. I really didn't think she'd pick up.

"Hello?"

"Hey."

"Hey."

Oh God, she doesn't recognize my voice and she's just pretending she knows who I am. Who does she think I am? Some other guy, some guy who calls her all the time, whose voice she would recognize. Maybe she has a boyfriend from another school.

"It's Nick," I say. I want to make sure that's clear.

"Yeah," she says. Maybe she did recognize my voice after all. "What's up, Nick?"

I'm up, I think. I'm standing up in my spot.

"Nothing much. How about you?"

"Arrr," she purrs, and I imagine that she's still in bed maybe, maybe she's exhausted from last night, too, maybe she's reaching her arms up over her head to stretch, and maybe as she does so, her shirt lifts up a little, exposing her midriff. I imagine her stomach white, whiter than her arms and legs, because she would wear a one-piece at the beach, one of those suits that look like they're from the 1950s. Her stomach would feel like a mattress with clean sheets pulled tightly over it, and it would be warm when I touched it.

"Just hanging out. Procrastinating, mostly," she says.

"What're you supposed to be doing?"

"Studying for Barsky's history quiz on Tuesday."

"Oh, yeah, I guess I'm supposed to be doing that, too."

"Yeah."

"Yeah," I echo. "So," I say, and as I say it, I take a step, outside of my spot, screwing up the whole scene. And then another step, and another, and then back, stepping back toward my spot, but then I step right through it, and on behind it. I'm pacing.

"So, how about we procrastinate together? Or maybe study together—tomorrow, after school?"

"Study?"

"Well, we'd have every intention of studying, of course."

"Of course." I imagine she's rolling over now, resting her chin on her hand, waiting to hear what else I have to say.

"But if we just happened to get distracted—"

"By what?" she interjects, and now I imagine that she's sitting up. Shit, did she think I was coming on to her? Or wait, did she like that I was coming on to her?

I mean, I don't want to not come on to her. But I shouldn't be too overt about it. And I certainly shouldn't do it accidentally, like I think I just did.

"Like, things that might come up." Shit, did I really just say things that might come up? I'm a walking cliché of bad, bad lines from bad, bad movies.

"Like, you know, meals that need to be eaten, highlighters that run out of ink. Paper cuts, which, you know, we could incur while studying, that would then have to be attended to."

"Studying can be fraught with danger," she says.

I think she's flirting with me. Halle-friggin-lujah.

"It can. Best not to do it alone."

"Absolutely."

"So, tomorrow, after school."

"Absolutely."

Well, now at least if I call Stevie, chances are I won't find time to say anything about Sam Roth.

After School

The subway is pretty crowded on the way down to Tribeca. Crowded enough that I stand while Eden sits. She can't cross her legs because that would take up too much space, so her feet are firmly on the ground. I stand with my legs on either side of hers, my hand on the metal bar above both of us so that I don't fall with every stop and start. I try not to look down her shirt; as much as I want to see her chest, this isn't exactly the way I had in mind. But I can't help seeing the edges of her bra, white and shiny, and even though I'm hanging on, my legs bang into hers at every stop, my knees hitting her thighs, and even through my khakis, I can feel the warmth of her bare legs. I want to hold her like that, my legs pressing on hers from either side, to show that she is mine; but she isn't, so I don't.

Before I met Eden in the school lobby today, Stevie pulled me aside to wish me luck. He stuck a handful of condoms in my backpack.

"Got these from the nurse's office for you," he said, patting my shoulder.

"You're an asshole," I said.

"You're blushing," he replied.

Eden's apartment is one of those where the elevator opens right into the apartment, but not like Stevie's, where it opens into a foyer where you see all this art with even a Rodin and a Miró that they inherited from his grandparents. The Reisses' elevator opens right into the living room, and you can see an open kitchen to the right, and the only artwork is huge framed photographs mounted on exposed-brick walls. It's kind of the cliché of a Tribeca loft, like from a movie about artists living in downtown Manhattan made by people who've never been to Manhattan. One of those movies that have scenes where something happens on East 59th Street and then a character has to take a cab to get to Bloomingdale's, which is on East 59th Street.

I've seen Eden's mother before, at school functions and things, but she's always dressed, obviously, when I see her, so I'm a little thrown by the woman walking toward us in flannel pajama pants and T-shirt. I notice that she's obviously not wearing a bra and her breasts swing with every step, but in a way that is so unattractive that for a second I actually worry about what Eden's boobs might look like without a bra, and I really hope they don't swing like that.

"Nick, right?" she says to me, and I nod, trying not to stare at her chest.

"How are you, Mrs. Reiss?"

"Becker, actually. My maiden name."

I nod. That happens with my mom all the time. She kept her maiden name, too—Ellerstein—and hates when people assume that her last name is Brandt.

"I used to use Reiss," she continues, "but I've decided I'm going back to Becker now."

I nod again. I don't actually want to ask why.

"Okay, Mom," Eden says, and I'm relieved she's taking control. "We have that history thing to study for, remember?"

"Yes, of course."

"Okay," Eden says, and turns to the right. I begin to follow her when Ms. Becker says, "Staying for dinner, Nick?"

I look at Eden. I don't know if I'm invited to stay for dinner. She hadn't mentioned that.

"We'll probably get pizza or something," Eden says, though I'm not sure if she's telling her mother that, or me.

"Because, you know, Nick, I might cook something, so I would just need to know how many people to cook for. Eden's father never tells us when he'll be home, and it's very annoying not to know for whom you are cooking."

I look at Eden again. Ms. Becker said "for whom you are

cooking" very slowly, with an emphasis on the words "whom" and "are."

"You never cook, Mom," Eden says finally. "If we decide to order something, I'll let you know, in case you want in on it."

Ms. Becker doesn't say anything. I think she's pretending not to hear. Eden starts walking again and I follow her into her room and she closes the door firmly behind her. My mother wouldn't let us do that, and even though I suspect it's more to do with the fact that Eden's mom isn't entirely, well, aware, I mostly just feel lucky that Ms. Becker isn't the kind of mom who notices when her daughter closes the door to her room with a boy on the other side of it.

"I'm sorry about that," Eden says.

"About what?" I say.

"Don't pretend to be clueless," she says, and she sounds angry at me.

I nod. I think how I would feel if my mother met one of my friends with her breasts swinging low and complained about my father, intimating that she was thinking of leaving him by changing her name. I don't think Eden is embarrassed; I think she's angry.

I say, "I'm sorry."

"Don't be sorry, either," she says, and sits down on the floor, leaning against her bed. I sit down next to her. I'm not touching her, but being this close to her makes my stomach hurt.

"Don't worry," she says, "you'll probably be gone before my dad gets home and their bickering begins. He works late. Later and later, actually. I don't blame him; I'd avoid it, too. I mean, I can't believe she said that, about changing her name."

"It's okay," I say, and then, realizing how condescending that sounds, I add, "I mean, I won't tell anyone about it."

"It doesn't matter." She shrugs. "I mean, anyone can tell by looking at them. They're not going to last much longer, or if they are, it certainly won't be any good."

"Oh?"

"You should hear the things she says when he does get home. You wouldn't know what to make of it. Nothing like that happens at your house." She says it like she knows it for a fact.

"What's that supposed to mean?" I say, and I'm surprised at how defensive I sound, like it's an insult that she thinks that my parents don't fight.

"Dude, your parents *hold hands* on parents' day."

"They do?"

"Yeah. You never noticed?"

I shrug.

"I saw them, sitting in the back of the room. Like this," she says, and she takes my hand in hers. "Your dad even squeezed her hand," she says, "like this," and she squeezes my hand. Maybe it's just my imagination, but my skin where she is touching me feels so hot that I can't believe she hasn't let go, like the way you'd drop a hot plate.

"I didn't know," I say, thinking only of the fact that she may be the only person, other than, say, my parents and my grandparents, whose hand I've held. Her skin is so soft it's almost slippery.

"I was watching them," she says, kind of wistfully, leaning her head back against her bed, loosening her grip on my hand, but not letting go.

I should say something. This is an opportunity. I mean, I've been in rooms alone with girls before. I've leaned toward them and kissed them, at parties, maybe snuck off to someone else's bedroom or even their bathroom, tried sticking my hands up a shirt or under a waistband. But being alone with Eden is nothing like that, and it certainly doesn't feel like a moment to make a move. Our hands are resting in the space between our legs, but loosely, like we've been holding each other's hands for years, like it's not a big deal. It doesn't even feel like she was really taking my hand, only that she was trying to show me something. But I should at least say something.

But she speaks first. "I guess we should study now, huh?" she says, and when she gets on her hands and knees to reach for her backpack, she drops my hand.

Chips & Salsa

I stay long enough that we eventually order pizza for dinner. Eden asks her mother if she wants any, and Ms. Becker says no; then when the pizza arrives, she eats more than half the pie, so Eden and I only get a slice and a half each. I leave hungry, just as, it turns out, her father gets home. He steps off the elevator as I'm about to get on it.

"Hi, Dad," Eden says. He's wearing gray pants and a blue shirt; I get the impression his closet is filled with rows of nothing but gray pants and blue shirts. He's tall, and he doesn't look so much at Eden or at me as he looks above our heads at the living room behind us. After a second of silence, Eden slides between his body and the wall to catch the elevator before the door can close.

"See you later, Nick," Eden says, and I step past her father, and past her, onto the elevator. Eden's hair looks especially dark as her father walks into the apartment behind us; I'm not sure if he noticed that Eden had a friend over. I hold Eden's gaze until the elevator door closes.

When I get home, I head straight for the kitchen. I find a bag of chips and a container of salsa, which I eat standing up, leaning over the kitchen counter.

"Don't you at least want to take off your backpack?" my dad says behind me.

"Jesus, Dad, you're gonna make a person choke, sneaking up like that."

"Sorry," he says, and he grabs the chips and salsa, carries them out of the kitchen and to the dining room table, and sits down. I slide my backpack off and leave it on the kitchen floor, then I follow him.

"Where's Mom?"

"Walking Pilot."

"Oh."

We sit there, eating our chips and salsa. It's a good thing I actually did end up studying a lot at Eden's house, because I'm not at all interested in studying now.

"What does Sam Roth's mother do now?" I say, lifting a chip to my mouth.

"What?" he says, though he doesn't sound surprised that I brought it up, doesn't even stop on his way to dip a chip into the salsa.

I wait a little before repeating my question, chew some more, and then swallow.

"Sam Roth's mom—what does she do?"

"Her name's Michelle. She's a high school principal. The school Sam graduated from, as a matter of fact."

I shake my head, reaching for another chip, like this will be a casual question. "No, I mean, his real mother. Your old girl-friend." I can't remember her name.

"Oh. I don't know."

"You don't know?"

"No. We lost touch after the baby was born. I assume she got married, left town, did what most people did."

"She might still be living in Troy?"

"I doubt it." I scratch the roof of my mouth, shoving a whole chip in. Ever since we got on this subject, I've been eating fast, like I'm starving. A piece of chip gets caught in my throat, with sharp edges, but I don't cough. If I did, Dad would get up, pat my back, tell me I should be more careful, take my time, and the rhythm of the conversation would be lost.

"But, like, we could bump into her when we visit Grandma and Grandpa this Christmas."

"No. I don't think so. She left Troy, I'm sure." Dad seems to have made up his mind to believe it.

"Doesn't Sam know where she lives?"

Dad shakes his head. "How would he?"

"Well, he called us."

"Oh. Sarah"—right, that's her name—"didn't put her name on the registry."

"The registry," I repeat, thinking of college registrar offices and presents for cousins' weddings bought off a registry.

"There's a registry," Dad says. "You can opt in to be found, if someone decides to look for you. But only after the child has turned eighteen."

"What made you decide to go onto the registry now?"

"Now?"

"Well, he's only just found us, so what made you decide to opt in now?"

Dad leans back now, places his hands on his stomach so that I know he's done eating.

"Actually, I signed up the very day Sam turned eighteen."

"Oh."

Dad doesn't say anything, and I can't decide which question to ask next. Finally, I say, "Well, why did he wait till now to call us?"

"He hadn't gone on the registry until this past summer."

"Right, so what made him decide to do it now, this summer?"

Dad pauses, smiles faintly. "He's getting married," he says, more an exhalation than a sentence. I can't tell, but it almost sounds like he's pleased, maybe even proud.

"But Sarah isn't on the registry."

"No."

"But he could find her now. I mean, you could tell him her whole name—what's her last name?"

Dad looks at me. I think he's actually considering not telling me this woman's name, as though I might go looking for her or something. As though he's forgotten that I certainly have no reason to try to find her.

"Sarah Booker," he says finally.

"Good name."

"Yes. A great name."

"Like a woman in a novel."

"Yeah. A 1920s novel with good honest words and good clear names."

"Ernest Hemingway," I suggest, and Dad nods.

"So why not tell Sam her name? He could find her now."

"He doesn't want to. He didn't even want to know her name."

"Why?"

Dad looks away from me now, up at the ceiling, like maybe the answer's stuck up there somewhere, like he threw it up behind the lights and all he has to do is reach around the bulb to get it down.

"It's hard for me to explain to you, Nick."

"Why? Seems like the natural next step, after finding you."

"That's just the thing, Nick—he didn't go out and find me. It's not as though he had to search for me. Essentially, by signing up on the registry, I gave him my name, I gave him my phone number, and I told him where I live."

"Okay."

"So, Sarah hasn't done that."

"Right, but now you can just tell him, and he doesn't need the registry."

I get up now, go back into the kitchen and toss the almost empty bag of chips, put the lid back on the salsa, put it in the fridge. Our kitchen is open, like Eden's, so from here, leaning against the countertop, I am looking straight at Dad sitting at the table. I can watch him talking slowly to me like I'm a little kid who can't understand anything.

"He doesn't need the registry anymore," I repeat.

Dad shakes his head. He's not looking at me.

"Sam thinks he does. He doesn't want to go after her like that. Her not registering is basically like her saying she doesn't want to know him, as far as Sam's concerned. And he doesn't want to meet her like that."

"Oh," I say, pushing away from the kitchen counter and standing up straight. "I think I'm going to get ready for bed now."

Dad nods, and I grab my backpack from the kitchen floor and walk past the dining room table toward my room without looking at him. I don't hear the sound of his chair being pushed away from the table, so I guess my dad is just sitting there, brushing chip crumbs from the stubble on his chin, waiting for Mom to come home with Pilot; when they walk this long, it usually means they've gone to the bookstore, and she comes home with new novels and magazines. My dad must be sitting there waiting, and thinking about Sarah Booker and Sam Roth.

I'm thinking of them now, and it's strange, I suppose, that I can't help thinking of them collectively even though they're two people who've never met each other, who don't even know one another's names. And I guess it's not really fair now that I know both of their names, when neither of them knows the other's.

I reach into my pocket for my cell phone and turn it on. I'd kept it turned off at Eden's house, 'cause I knew Stevie'd be texting me something ridiculous. Now I can see that Stevie has sent me no fewer than eight text messages. I scroll through them.

> 1: Don't get lost on your way to Tribeca.
> 2: Eden Eden bo beden banana fana fo feden me mi mo meden Eden.
> 3: I hope you guys are studying at least a little cause dude you do not want a bad grade on this sucker.
> 4: Sorry, that last message was insensitive. You get very good grades.
> 5: What color is Eden's bra today?
> 6: Matching panties?
> 7: Jesus I hate the word panties.
> 8: Hope the rest of your night is okay.

I take a second look at that eighth one—no way did Stevie send something so harmless. It's from Eden. Shit. I should write back, like right now. She might have sent this the minute I left her apartment, which was well over an hour ago, and now she thinks I'm an asshole not to have written her back, I bet.

I hit reply.

> Hey—just got your message. My phone was off. Thanks for studying.
> Hopefully we're ready for the test.

What am I, writing a novel? I delete everything but "hey."

Couldn't be better than the beginning of my night—

Delete. That sounds creepy, not flirty.

Finally, I write:

Hey—thanks. You too.

I hit send. I should call Stevie, but I really don't feel like talking; I don't want to tell about Eden's mother's breasts and the way she introduced herself, or about the way Eden took my hand and have to explain that it wasn't the right time to make a move. I don't want to say that I only had a little bit of pizza and that I had to come home and snack, and I definitely do not want to think about, let alone talk about, talking to my dad over chips and salsa.

So I just text Stevie that I'm crashing, and that he's a loser, and that I'll see him tomorrow and I plan to smoke his sorry ass on the quiz.

It is much, much easier to text Stevie than to text Eden. When I can't fall asleep, I double-check to make sure that I didn't accidentally hit reply to the wrong message so that what was meant for Stevie somehow made its way to Eden.

Smooth

"**S**o, touched the forbidden fruit yet?"

"Huh?" I'm leaning against my locker; Stevie's leaning against the locker to my right. We're both looking straight ahead.

"Notice that I said touch, not tasted, buddy."

"Yeah, I noticed."

"What time'd you get home last night?"

"I don't know . . . around nine."

"Dude, you didn't text me till, like, ten-thirty."

"I was talking to my dad."

"Oh." I feel the lockers shifting behind me, and I guess

Stevie is twisting to face me, but I don't turn. "You know, he looked terrible this morning. How's the market treating him?"

"Huh?"

"This morning, when your mom fed me breakfast? Your dad looked like he hadn't slept in ages."

"Yeah, I know."

"Everything okay, then?"

"Yeah. He's just, you know, got a lot on his mind."

"To say nothing of wondering whether his little boy has had any luck with the apple tree."

"You know . . ." A third voice enters the conversation, and the lockers give under some new weight leaning on them. I turn and I'm horrified to see Eden leaning back on the other side of Stevie. How long has she been there—and seriously, how much has she heard?

"You know, Stevie," she says, "there's nothing in the Bible to suggest it was an apple."

"Oh?"

"Nope. That's a pretty modern convention."

"Wouldn't be the first thing people just made up out of that book," Stevie says.

"How'd you know that?" I ask Eden, hating Stevie for the easy way he's lapsed comfortably into conversation with Eden. He didn't even seem thrown to find her on his right side.

"Dude, you think there's anything about Eden I haven't heard? Gotta know your facts with a name like this."

"Oh, I hear you," Stevie says. "Imagine all the crap that gets hurled at guys with names like Steven and Nicholas."

"I can only dream."

"Nightmares, baby, nightmares."

Eden giggles. I've never heard her giggle. She's not really a giggling type of girl.

"Well, I'm gonna get to class," Stevie says, leaning down to pick up the bag at his feet. "Don't want to be late for that quiz."

I glance at my watch, peeling myself off my locker to stand up straight.

"We still have fifteen minutes," I say to Stevie's back. Maybe the battery in my watch has died and really I'm running late and I didn't even know it.

Stevie turns back and grins at me, then shrugs at Eden.

"Try to toss a friend some help," he says, and walks away.

Crap. I hate that Stevie thinks I need his help—worse yet, I hate that I do need his help.

Eden slides along the lockers toward me. Her long brown hair seems to move more slowly than the rest of her, trails behind her on the lockers as she moves.

"Stevie's pretty smooth," she says, nodding in his direction.

"Yeah."

"Wonder what he's trying to cover up."

"Huh?"

"Anyone that smooth has something to hide, right?"

I think about telling her about Stevie's parents, about his coming on all my family vacations, about the fact that he's slept every Christmas Eve since we were five on the floor of my bedroom, and how my parents still sign our presents from Santa Claus. My parents even tell us that the checks that Stevie's parents give us are from Santa, even though their names are obviously on them and we know who they're from. (And even though we're both technically Jewish. And too old to believe in Santa Claus.) When we leave for Ohio on Christmas Day, Stevie is always waving from the curb, Pilot at his side since he watches Pilot for us while we're gone. I'm pretty sure that's the only trip we take that Stevie's not tacitly—or explicitly—invited to join. I mean, Jesus, my parents may infantilize me—Stevie, too, when they get the chance—but mostly, at least, they stick around.

But instead of saying any of that, I say, "You're pretty smooth, too."

Eden looks down, and her hair falls over her face. I can smell her shampoo: grapefruit and brown sugar.

I realize I've implied that she's hiding something, too. "Sorry," I say quickly.

Eden shrugs. I try to make it better with a joke at my own expense.

"Well, if how smooth you are is a measure of what you have to hide, I guess I've got nothing."

Eden looks up at me now, and smiles.

"Oh, I don't know, Nick. You've got some moves."

"Yeah?"

"Yeah."

I smile. "I guess everyone has something to hide."

"I guess so."

Eden leans down to pick up her bag.

"Ready for the quiz?" I say.

"Let's just get it over with," she says, and we head for the classroom. And as we walk, just for a second, I put my left hand on her right shoulder. Her skin is hot underneath her shirt.

After school, Eden joins Stevie and me outside the pizza shop, now crowded with students. It feels comfortable with her here, staring at the middle schoolers, and pointing out to Stevie which of the senior girls roll their uniform skirts so high you can see their boy shorts underneath. And it even feels natural when she leans back against me, rather than against the pizza-place wall.

"Dirty," she explains, pointing at the wall, like I'm the obvious alternative.

"Glad to help keep you clean," I answer. I feel stronger, somehow, with her weight against my chest.

And as she leans on me, her left hand brushes mine, and it feels perfectly natural to me that I should take that hand. She looks up and smiles at me, and I feel distinctly like right now I'm exactly where I'm supposed to be, outside my school on a New York City fall day with my best friend beside me and—forgive the cliché—my best girl's hand in mine.

I walk Eden to the subway, and the whole walk there, I know I'm going to kiss her good-bye, and I know she's going to kiss me back. I feel the kiss coming up from my stomach, as though that's where every kiss originates, waiting in your belly, growing stronger as it climbs up your rib cage, fluttering a bit when it passes your heart, and waiting, patiently in your throat, until you tilt your head and move your lips, and it knows it's time to come out from inside you.

Eden probably knows I'm just waiting for the subway stop

to kiss her; she's waiting for it. And so I decide to use one of those moves she said I had. A block before the subway stop, I take her hand and pull her so that I'm leaning against a building and she's facing me, and then I kiss her. I press her hands onto my sides until she takes hold of my shirt on either side of me. I don't stick my tongue down her throat or anything. I mean, there's some tongue involved. But not at first. First I kiss her once, quickly, and then again for a little bit longer. The taste of her is completely new, everything I imagined—the apples, the honey—and a thousand other things I never knew a person could taste like. I move my hands so that they're on her hips, and I pull them toward me, my fingertips just barely resting on the curve of her ass. And then I pull her even closer and lean down over her and really kiss her. And then there's tongue, and breath and warmth. And I know that I would never, not in a million years, be kissing her like this with my hands in those places, if she hadn't told me that I had moves, that I was smooth.

The Implications of Smooth

Later, walking home by myself, I'm thinking about Eden's theory that people who are smooth have something to cover up. And I can see how that makes sense. Stevie has his ridiculously busy parents, and, from what I can tell, Eden's home life isn't so great, either. And neither of them ever talks about those things; instead they're both smart and quick on the uptake. They're always ready with a great comeback and a snappy joke, cleverness coming out of them so fast and easy it practically falls from their mouths.

Where do I fit into Eden's theory? Up until a week ago, my

family life was what both Stevie and Eden would call idyllic; we fight, but no one's changing her name, and no one's getting ignored. But up until a week ago, I barely had the nerve to talk to Eden, and I certainly never would have had the nerve to pull her to the side of the street and kiss her for twenty minutes.

Maybe I should call up Sam Roth. Or at least send him a thank-you note: Thank you for fucking up my life enough that I got to be smooth for at least one afternoon. And it occurs to me then that I don't know where he lives. I know he grew up in Texas, sure, but he might not still live there. My dad grew up in Ohio and moved away as soon as he finished high school, pretty much.

"What're you smiling about?" my dad asks me later, during the boring part of *Jeopardy!* when they ask the contestants about their lives. I had been thinking about how chapped my lips were.

"Thinking about how I'm going to kick your ass at *Jeopardy!* today." We're sitting on the couch, both of us in jeans and T-shirts, with our feet up on the coffee table and Pilot in between us. Mom's in the other room, on the phone. I can tell Dad doesn't believe that it's *Jeopardy!* that's got me smiling, so I change the subject, because I don't want to tell him about Eden.

"Any word from Sam Roth today?"

"Sorry?"

"You heard me," I say, but I am careful to sound friendly, casual.

"Not today, no. He and his fiancée left for vacation on Monday." It seems very strange that he knows that, like Sam Roth is a really good friend who always lets you know when he's leaving town so that you don't worry when you don't hear from him for a few days.

"Where'd they go?"

"Montana, I think."

"Montana? That's kind of random."

"There's some fancy camping resort. They like to go camping."

I wonder just how much my dad knows about Sam Roth. How well he knows him. I wonder if he's keeping track of the facts, the way I am: he's from Texas, he's getting married, he likes camping.

They're starting to ask questions on the show again, but I can tell Dad's only pretending to be watching now.

"I wonder how he told his fiancée about you."

"I think she always knew he was adopted. He said he wasn't raised to keep it a secret."

"Oh."

"Yeah."

Well, that's stupid, I think. Not that he was raised not to keep it a secret, but Dad's having said that his fiancée always knew he was adopted. Not possible. It's not like he picked her up at some bar and said, Hi, my name's Sam Roth, and I'd like to ask you out and by the way before I do I'd like to tell you that I also happen to be adopted. I mean, he would have told her at some point while they were dating. She can't have always known.

Dad looks straight at the TV when he answers my questions,

and I know he wants me to just play the game with him, but I have more things to ask.

"You were."

"What?"

"You were raised to keep it a secret."

He looks at me now.

"It's not exactly the same thing."

"It is exactly the same thing."

He opens and then shuts his mouth. He looks back at the TV. I reach for the remote and hit the mute button.

"You kept it a secret."

"There were people who knew."

"Who?"

"Well, I told my mother. And your uncle Hank."

"And Sarah's family?"

He shakes his head. "I don't know who Sarah ever told. We didn't talk about it."

"Would have been hard to keep a secret, though, right? I mean, she looked pregnant, right?"

Dad shrugs. "I honestly don't know, Nick." I remember he wasn't there during most of her pregnancy; he was away at college.

"How about Mom?" I press. "When did you tell her?"

He's still looking straight ahead. I suspect he's reading the clues on the screen.

"I don't remember, actually. While we were dating."

"When you were dating?"

"Yes. I couldn't exactly be talking to your mother about getting married and starting our own family without letting her know about him."

"You couldn't?"

He looks at me, as if surprised to find that I don't completely understand that. And I look back, because I want him to know that of course I understand it, but I'm coming around to a point here.

"No," he says slowly, "I could not."

"And did you tell her when you put your name on the registry?"

"Of course. She was with me when I did it."

"She was?"

"Yes. I mean, it's just a button on the computer. But yes, she stayed with me while I did it, she sat next to me, at the table there." He nods in the direction of the dining room table. I wonder when they did it. Maybe while I was at school. But what if his eighteenth birthday fell on a weekend; maybe they got up early, did it before I was even awake, sneaking around in the dark.

"And did you tell Grandma and Uncle Hank?"

"I think I must have. I mean, I don't know if I told them when I did it, but they knew I was planning on doing it, once Sam turned eighteen."

"So, you told all these people. Because you didn't think it would be honest not to tell them."

Dad nods. "I don't think I could have gone through it without telling them." I think he still doesn't see where I'm headed.

"So, you owed all that honesty to Mom and to your family, but you didn't think that maybe you owed it to me?"

"What?"

I swing my feet off the coffee table and sit up with them on the floor in front of me. I suddenly wish I were wearing shoes. "When you registered—you didn't think maybe you should have warned me, Hey, son there's a chance the phone might ring some day and it'll be this kid I kinda sorta used to know?" I say it meanly, purposely doing a bad imitation of my father's voice, mocking the sort of middle-America country twang that comes out in his voice from time to time.

"Nick," Dad says, sitting up also, genuinely surprised. "You were five years old when I registered."

"I was completely left out when you registered. A whole part of your life—of *our* life—that you didn't think to include me in."

"You were left out?" Dad repeats.

"Yes. And maybe I was five then," I continue, standing up now, "but didn't it occur to you in the eleven years between then and now that I might have gotten old enough to handle it? You and Mom always treat me like I'm so much younger than I am. One of these days you're going to have to notice that I've grown up a little bit since I was five friggin' years old."

"Well, you certainly could have fooled me," Dad says. This is probably the part when other kids' parents would be yelling, but my dad doesn't yell, and doesn't even stand up but keeps his feet firmly on the floor. I look jealously at his shoes. "I mean that you're not five anymore. All evidence to the contrary, Nicholas."

I look down at him, and then I look at Pilot, whose ears are standing straight up on alert. He's not used to hearing us speaking like this. We're not yelling, but I know we sound angry. He keeps looking at my father and back to me for a clue about what this all means. I can't think of anything to say, so I just look at Pilot.

Finally, I say, "You've upset the dog," and I turn on my heel to walk to my room, as though upsetting Pilot was the end result of the conversation.

And maybe it was. Because I don't really understand why I'm so upset. Why should I be angry at my dad for having had Sam Roth almost thirty years ago?

⁓

Eden answers on the fourth ring, just when I'd begun to think she was screening me, when I'd begun to curse the people who invented caller ID because I would have to leave a message or else she'd know I'd called and hung up.

"Hey, Nick."

"Hi, Eden."

"What's up?"

"Are you chewing gum?"

"Yes," she answers unapologetically, and pops a few bubbles for effect.

"You sure do chew gum a lot."

"It's a little creepy that you just admitted you've been look-ing at my mouth."

"Nah, I think it just shows I'm observant."

"You're something."

"Or other."

Now that I've been in her room, I can really picture her there. Maybe she was sitting at her desk when I called, and now she's getting up, bare feet cold on the floor, taking steps toward the bed, on the edge of which she perches, crosses her legs. Maybe she raises her hand to touch her lips, remembering how I kissed her.

"What's up, Nick?"

This whole time I've been pacing, walking back and forth across my room, which is not at all that large and it really only takes me a few steps, and I actually, for a second, wish that I were shorter, or at least that my legs were shorter, so that it would take me longer to cross the room. Usually I'm very grateful for my long legs, for the extra few inches they give me, the extra inches that allowed me to lean my head down over Eden's this afternoon instead of just look her in the face. I get the long legs from my mom. My dad's pretty short and, shit, now I'm busy wondering how tall Sam Roth is instead of talking to Eden.

"Nick?"

"Yeah, sorry." I stop walking and sit on my bed, just at the edge like really it's someone else's bed and I'm scared to disturb it.

"Are you mad at your parents?" I say finally.

"What?"

"Are you mad, at your parents, you know, at your mom, for the way she was the other night, talking about your dad in front of me, eating our pizza?"

"Wow. And here I thought you were just calling to secure a second make-out session. One kiss is a little early for delving this deep, don't you think, Nick?"

"It wasn't just one kiss," I say, my voice dropping an octave. There it is again, this newfound smoothness. Awesome. But I don't want to get offtrack here. "I just thought I'd skip over all that awkwardness, and assume you were in for a long haul of countless make-out sessions, and go straight to the good, deep, adolescently-angst-ridden-let's-rail-against-our-parents stuff."

"Well, since you put it that way—hang on." I can hear her put the phone down and I imagine she's walking across her bedroom. When she comes back, she says, "Had to spit out my gum."

"Oh, wow, we really are getting to the good stuff."

"Yes, I am."

"Am what?"

"It was your question, Nick."

"Angry at them?"

"Yes. But only sometimes."

"Why only sometimes?"

"'Cause, I mean, I guess I'm used to it. I mean, I only realized how creepy they are recently."

"What do you mean?"

"I don't know. For most of my life, I didn't know other parents were different from them."

"No?"

"I didn't know parents could be any other way—I didn't know parents could be like yours."

I don't want to tell her what my parents are like, what my dad is really like, now.

"And your parents were always like that?" I ask.

"Kinda. I mean, the hating of one another is fairly recent, and I don't expect that to last that long, but yeah, they were always weird."

"What do you mean, you don't expect it to last that long?"

"I figure they'll either get over it or get divorced."

"You say that pretty casually."

I imagine her stretching now, lying back on her bed to think about it, just like I'm doing right now.

"I don't know. Are kids even allowed to get upset when our parents get divorced nowadays?"

"You're the only girl I've ever met who'd ever say the word 'nowadays' as if she'd been around since before."

"Since before what?"

"I don't know. Since before nowadays."

"My mom says I'm an old soul."

"Not sure exactly what that means."

"I think it means I'm wise beyond my years," she says, and I swear I can see her smile across the phone line, her tongue peeking out from between her teeth. Though then her tone changes. "Of course, that's the same woman who literally can't decide what she wants for dinner until food is placed in front of her, and then she gets incredibly furious that you didn't get her what she wanted."

I laugh.

"Was it hugely rude of me to tell you I noticed how weird your mom is?"

"Yes, but I don't care. It's not like hers is a subtle weirdness. At least you're honest."

"I try."

"What made you ask, though?"

"What?"

"If I'm angry at my parents."

I shrug, then remember she can't see me, so I say, "I don't know. I think I might be angry at mine." My tongue feels thick in my mouth, and I wonder why this is hard to say.

"Not for the regular shit, you know, like giving me a hard time about ditching them for dinner or not wearing a scarf when my mother thinks it's cold out. Like, really angry. Like, for something big, something more—I don't know. Just angry at them—overall."

I think Eden is nodding.

"I never felt like that before," I say.

"Really?"

"No. I mean, it's not like they're perfect or anything . . ."

"The rest of the junior class begs to differ."

I smile. "Ha. Well, anyway. It's just different now. Bigger."

"You gonna tell me why?"

"No. Not yet. I still like that you think my parents are perfect."

"Nobody's perfect."

"So I'm beginning to realize." Except you, I want to say.

"Some people, I think you just have to know them better before you find out."

"I guess. I just never thought I didn't know my parents before."

"Yeah."

"Yeah." I sit up and rub my eyes. I'm scared if I don't get off the phone with her soon I'll tell her about Sam Roth, even though I decided that I wouldn't.

"I better go call Stevie before he begins to wonder what happened this afternoon. He'll start a rumor that I followed you home and you had to call the cops on me."

"That's pretty extreme."

"Not for Stevie. It'd be the only reason he'd be able to come up with for why I couldn't call him."

"You get one phone call in jail, don't you?"

"Yeah, but even Stevie would know that I'd probably have to use it to call my parents. Or a lawyer."

"Right."

"Right."

"Good night."

"Good night."

I like to think that maybe I'm the last person she'll have talked to before she goes to sleep tonight.

My Girlfriend

❧

My girlfriend has thick brown hair and skinny white legs and a dark brown freckle hidden behind her right knee.

Every weekday morning she meets Stevie and me, and together we lean against the pizza place and watch the underclassmen and feel infinitely superior. Then Stevie goes inside, and Eden and I sneak around the corner and kiss until our lips are sore, or until we realize that we're going to be late for class.

Stevie even says "here" for both of us in homeroom to buy us an extra few minutes before first period. Somehow, the teachers have yet to catch on to Stevie's high-pitched impression of Eden's voice.

Eden's kisses are always different; I make a joke that they're like snowflakes, no two quite the same. There's always the familiar taste and feel of her, but it changes depending on her mood, on the time of day, on whether it's sunny or cold outside. When we kiss in the rain, her face is slippery under my fingers.

On Friday nights, we go to the movies, even though I joke that that makes us like kids growing up in the suburbs thirty years ago. I want to ask my dad whether that's actually what he did on Friday nights when he was in high school, but I can't, since I'd first have to tell him about Eden, and I'm not telling him about Eden yet.

Eden says it can't really be all that suburban an experience since we take subways and try to go to theaters not on the Upper West Side so that we won't bump into all the kids from school. We go to the enormous movie theaters in Times Square with the tourists, to the smaller ones below 14th Street that play independent movies, and to the one on West 23rd Street where both of us can't help noticing we're among the minority of straight couples there.

We don't make out in movie theaters because Eden says that would be a waste of the exorbitant ticket prices. I say that I am worth significantly more than eleven dollars and fifty cents, and when she laughs at me in the dark theater, her teeth are so white they almost glow. We don't make out but we hold hands, and Eden's fingers are so short that when they interlace with mine, they barely hit my knuckles. This makes me feel tall.

After the movies, we go for dinner or drinks, and sometimes Stevie is with us. It's colder now, and Eden is always stealing my scarf, and I complain but I actually like it, my scarf like some Northeastern version of a pin so people know that we're a couple. When she hands it back to me, it always smells like her, sweet but smoky, and once I fell asleep holding it, like a child's stuffed animal or a security blanket. And when I sleep, I have dreams that she is kissing my hands.

I keep saying that I'm going to get her a scarf for Christmas, because at this rate my neck'll barely make it through the cold of the new year. And Eden says I better come up with something less prosaic than a scarf, and that makes me happy because not only does it mean that my girlfriend uses words like "prosaic," but it also means she thinks we'll stay together at least through Christmas. Even though the latter is a totally girly thing of me to think. Maybe the former, too, come to think of it. When I told Stevie, he said, "Dude, you are so gay."

"That's a slur," I said.

"You're a slur."

"Stellar comeback."

"No, actually, you're right, that is a slur. I would never want to imply that the homosexual community could possibly be as lame as you are."

"Well, I'm sure the homosexual community thanks you."

But I'm not ashamed of my rather lame thoughts and moments; my girlfriend deserves each one. My girlfriend knows all kinds of big words, and in addition to the novels we read for school, she likes to read all kinds of nonfiction in her free time, biographies of American presidents and books about the history of the food we eat and the clothes we wear. She's a much faster (or maybe slightly more careless) worker than I am, so in the afternoons at her house, when I'm still doing homework, she's usually reading books like that. She goes through at least one a week.

We always go to her house after school. I tell my parents I'm going to a friend's house, and maybe they think I'm at Stevie's, or maybe someone else's entirely, but I don't think they know I've got a girlfriend. On the nights I stay at Eden's for dinner, her mother eats with us, and her father never gets there before the table has long since been cleared. Dinner is always delivery; Eden rolls her eyes when her mother mentions cooking because she knows it'll never happen.

Eden's parents mostly leave us alone. Her mother doesn't say anything when we close the door to Eden's room, and her father doesn't seem to register that his daughter has been spending all that much time with the same boy. Eden doesn't talk about it, and so I don't, either. I think we're both secretly pleased that they're too self-absorbed to notice us, because it gives us privacy. I guess I shouldn't be keeping track, but behind Eden's closed bedroom door I've gotten my hand down her pants at least seventeen times. I stopped counting after ten, so I'm guessing at the number here. And I can't even remember how many times I've touched her breasts, heard the sharp intake of breath when her nipples get hard. But she always makes sure we finish our homework, too.

～

Next week is Thanksgiving and on Wednesday, Eden says we should study at my house instead.

"Why?" I ask, standing beside her open locker and lacing my fingers through hers.

She unhooks her fingers in order to reach into her locker for some books.

"We always go to my house."

"Your house is better."

"Why on earth is my house better?"

"Who on earth says things like 'why on earth'?"

"The type of people who date people who don't want the people they're dating to come to their houses, apparently."

"That's some pretty serious sentence structure you've got going on."

"And this is a pretty serious conversation I'm trying to have."

"You are?" I ask; I honestly hadn't realized we were being all that serious.

"Yes, I am."

"Oh," I say, standing up straight now.

Then neither of us says anything.

"Okay, I want to be a good boyfriend and everything but I really don't know what the serious conversation you want to have is about."

"It's about us doing homework at your house today, you moron."

"See, you're trying really hard to be pissy with me, but you're failing miserably."

"I am pissy," she says, reaching into her locker for another book.

I shake my head. "Nope, sorry—pissy people are able to stop grinning when they call someone a moron."

Eden puffs out her bottom lip, pretending to pout; I don't think I've ever seen her actually pout, and come to think of it, I can't imagine her doing it. I focus on the fullness of her lip. She never needs to wear lipstick since her lips are naturally a dark, dusky pink.

"Well, you are a moron," she says finally.

"Well, you picked me, so what does that make you?"

Eden closes her locker and leans against it, hefting her bag up on her shoulder. She grins at me. "Nick, don't kid yourself. We know who picked who here."

"Whom," I correct her. But I'm thinking, Yes we do, and praise Jesus that I picked this girl.

⁓

I can't remember whether my dad was working from home today. Maybe he won't be home at all. Maybe neither of them will. I don't know if they'd let us close the door to my room. I think I just don't want to bother telling them that I have a girlfriend.

Pilot greets us at the door—a good sign; when someone's home, he doesn't usually run to the front door when it opens. Eden crouches down to pet him but he turns his back to her.

"He's pretty shy with new people," I say.

"I see that," she says, since after he rejects her he comes over

and leaps on me, and when I don't lean down he settles for licking my knees through my pants.

"Anyway," I say, unwinding my scarf and taking off my coat.
I reach for hers and begin to put both coats on the back of the
chairs in the dining room, but then I change my mind and keep
walking toward my own room, thinking I'll put them on my
desk chair instead.

"Come see my room," I say, my back to her.

"So much for the grand tour," she says, putting her arms
around me from behind.

"Not much to see," I say, and then I turn around to face her,
lean my lips down toward hers. But instead of kissing her, I say,
"That place by the door with the big, shiny humming appliances
was the kitchen, and the table and chairs to my right make up
the dining room, and the sofa to my left is in the living room."

"Very nice," Eden says, and now I take her hand, leading her
down the hallway that leads to the bedrooms.

"That room on the left is the guest room, and down on the
other end is my parents' room."

"And right smack in between?" Eden says, her lips close to
my ear.

"My room," I say, opening the door, and dropping her
hand now to step inside. She's going to be the first girl ever
to have stepped foot in here, I guess, not counting, you know,
elementary-school playdates, before girls became icky, and long
before icky became attractive.

Eden stands in the doorway, watching me put our coats on
my desk chair. She doesn't fully step inside the room.

"You coming in?"

She shakes her head, and her hair falls out of its ponytail. A piece sticks to her lip, and I walk over to her and brush it away.

"I'm enjoying the tour," she says.

I grin and take her hand. "This is my desk," I say, pulling her toward it. "This computer, believe it or not, is where I nightly compose those emails that put you to sleep all weak in the knees."

"All that at this little desk?" she asks, mock incredulously.

"Hard to believe, I know." I turn to face the window. "This is the window, out of which I stare when I am pretending to study and really just procrastinating."

"Fascinating," she says, like she's a scientist studying me. I imagine her with a Dictaphone, or taking notes.

"These are my bookshelves."

"And how are your books organized?"

I think about it for a minute, and she continues, "Alphabetically? Color-coded? By subject?"

"Nah," I say finally, "sequentially."

"What's that mean?"

"Like this shelf, for example." I point to the second shelf from the bottom. "Every single book we had to read in middle-school English."

She crouches down. "I see."

"And this shelf is all the reading I did in the summer between ninth and tenth grade," I say, pointing to the third from the bottom.

"Did you really do that on purpose?" she says, standing up, genuinely interested.

I smile and shake my head. "Nah, I just put them on the shelves from the bottom up as soon as I finished them."

"And now our tour continues," I say, taking back her hand. "You'll notice that the bookshelves are at the foot of another piece of furniture."

I can tell Eden's trying not to laugh. "I hadn't noticed, as a matter of fact."

"Well, good, because I'd like to explain this piece in particular."

"Really? Why?"

I start backing her up toward my bed, and I think that tonight her scent will be on my sheets. "See, up here there are these soft, fluffy objects."

"And what are they called?"

"You'll find them in most every boy's bedroom."

"Just boys'?"

"I don't pretend to be an expert on girls' rooms," I say, finally leaning over her so that we're lying on the bed, her head on my pillows.

"My bed's bigger than yours," she says as I rest my hips on top of hers, enjoying the feeling of her bones pressing against me, my face hovering above hers.

"Yet another reason your room is better."

"My books are organized by subject," she adds as I begin to kiss her neck, concentrating on the space just above her collarbone. When she sighs, I think I'm going to shiver.

"Really?"

"Yup." She puts her arms around my neck. "And my floor is carpeted."

"I did notice that."

"I'll bet," she says, smiling, and I know she's thinking of all the times we've messed around on her floor. I certainly am.

This is the first time I've made out with a girl in my own bed, and I think with anyone but Eden, it might feel strange. As I kiss her, I say, "I like the way you look in my room."

"Me too," she says, smiling, and she runs her left hand down my torso, and I inhale sharply when her fingers come to rest on my crotch, moving lightly along my fly.

"Shit," I say suddenly, almost falling down on top of her.

"What?" she says, moving her hand away.

"The front door just opened."

"You've got good ears," she says, and swings her legs over the side of my bed, straightening her uniform.

"They've got good timing," I say, because I'm sure both my parents have just walked in the door. I exhale heavily. I look at our coats twisted together on the back of my chair. I guess I brought them in here so my parents wouldn't guess someone else was here with me. Fat lot of good that did.

"You think they'll like me?" she asks, standing up. She actually sounds nervous. All I can think is that my parents don't even deserve to meet a girl who is sexy one minute and shy the next; all I can think is that I'm already in love with her.

"They'll love you," I say, taking her hand and leading her toward the door. "Come on."

Introductions

"**H**ey, guys," I say, coming out into the living room, Eden slightly behind but holding my hand. They're both bending down over the dog.

"Hi, sweetie," my mother says.

"She may have meant me, she may have meant Pilot. We'll never know," I stage-whisper to Eden, who grins.

"Huh?" my mom says, and they both look up now.

"This is Eden Reiss," I say as they stand up; the introduction sounds short without the words "my girlfriend" before her name. Eden drops my hand, which only serves to point out that we were holding hands to begin with, and takes a step toward my parents. When she leaves my side, I can still feel warmth coming from where she stood.

"Nice to meet you," she says, and shakes my mother's hand. "Nina."

My mother looks taken aback; I'm not sure if it's at meeting Eden or because Eden called her by her first name. My mother always corrects people when they call her Mrs. Brandt—first she says, Actually, it's Ms. Ellerstein, and then she says, Call me Nina. But she's used to my friends saying Mrs. and Mr. Brandt first.

"Rob," Eden continues, shaking my father's hand. Then she takes three steps backward, almost falling into me.

"Nice to meet you, Eden," my parents say practically in unison. I wonder whether Eden thinks the unison speech patterns chart up there with their having held hands on parents' day.

"Okay," I say finally. Now I wish I hadn't held Eden's hand when we came out here. I could have kept up a pretense that we were just friends, and we were just studying together.

"Well, Eden," my mother says. "That's an unusual name."

"Yes, well, my parents are unusual," Eden says, and she laughs, and my mother does, too.

"Before I forget, honey," my mother says, turning to me, "are Stevie's parents coming for Thanksgiving next week?"

Stevie always comes to our house for Thanksgiving, and when they're in town, his parents come, too. That sounds like they abandon him on Thanksgiving; they don't. In theory, he's supposed to go with them wherever they go, and he always did, until the year we were ten. For some reason, their trip was canceled at the last minute and we invited them here. Ever since

then, Stevie's opted out of traveling with his parents and spent
the holiday with us. His parents have only come once since then,
I think. But my mother always asks.

"No, they're going to Aspen, I think."

"A little early for skiing," my dad says. I think that's the first
thing he's said since I introduced Eden.

"I don't think they even ski," I say, shrugging. "There was
some restaurant there that had a special Thanksgiving dinner
thing they wanted to do."

"You're kidding," my mother says. She takes off her coat and
reaches for my dad's, and I realize they've been standing in their
own home for about ten minutes now with their coats still on.

"Anyway—" I say, ready to say something like, Eden and I
have to go back and get some more studying done.

"What's your family doing for Thanksgiving, Eden?" my
mother interrupts.

"Um, I honestly don't know," Eden says, and I look at her,
surprised.

"You don't?" I ask.

She shakes her head. "We usually go to this other couple's,
these friends of my mom's, but they're getting divorced now
so—"

"Your parents are getting divorced?" I interrupt.

Eden looks at me like I'm plain stupid.

"No, the other couple is."

"Sorry." Come on, it's not the most far-fetched thought in
the world.

"Anyway. So I don't know. We might skip it this year."

My parents look completely heartbroken. I mean, you'd think Eden had just intentionally stomped on Pilot's foot or something. Thanksgiving is a very big deal in our house. My parents have been spending the holiday together since they first started dating, even though sometimes that just meant the two of them and fifteen pounds of leftover turkey. I know they think I should invite Eden, and I know they're both surprised I haven't yet.

And even though that seems like a lot of family togetherness, I still say, "Well, you should come here. If your parents are going to skip it."

"Oh, I don't want to—"

"If your parents won't mind, Eden," my father breaks in, "we'd love to have you."

Eden smiles at my dad, in that big, warm way she doesn't do very often, and I can tell my dad, at least, thinks I did a good job catching this girl.

"Okay, great, then," I say. "Well, Eden and I were studying, so . . ."

"Yeah, midterms," Eden says. "Your son is a big help."

"I'll bet," my dad says, and I can't tell if he's joking.

I close the door behind us, though I'm not sure why since I can't imagine messing around now that my parents are home. It never bothers me when Eden's parents are home at her house. And I'm surprised that I feel this way about it now.

"Well, that went well," I say.

"Yeah," she says, and I can tell there's something else on her mind.

"What's the matter?" I say, even though I kind of don't want to know. I mean, I want to be, you know, a good boyfriend and everything, but also have absolutely no desire to get into anything right now.

"Nothing," she says, and I think she feels the same way I do; she doesn't want to get into anything, but she's also upset about something.

"You can tell me." I wonder if my parents did something wrong.

"Umm. Listen." She sits on the edge of my bed. "Your mother didn't know who I was."

I'm still standing up. "Well, she'd never met you before."

"Yeah, I realize that. I'm not an idiot, Nick. But she'd never heard my name before."

"What do you mean?"

"She said, 'Eden, that's an unusual name'—like she'd never heard it before."

I open and close my mouth three times before saying, "Yeah, I know," and sinking down on the bed next to her. "I know."

"Well, we've been dating for two months now, and my parents certainly know you."

"Well, we never come here," I say, regretting it the minute I say it, since it just underlines her point.

"I know," she says, and she stands up.

"You're angry," I say.

"No, I'm not," she says, running her fingers through her hair, which fell completely out of its ponytail when we were messing around, and walking toward my window. "Not exactly."

"I'm sorry."

"What for?"

"For not telling them about you. For not inviting you here before. I really am. I just, I wasn't, it had nothing to do with you. I honestly didn't think about how that might make you feel."

"What were you thinking about?"

"Come on, you've got to be impressed with the maturity and insight of that apology," I say, trying to bring back our normal banter.

"What were you thinking about?" she repeats, insistent now.

"I wasn't thinking."

"Sure you were," she says, and now I stand up, too.

"Sure I was. But"—I take a step toward her, an effort that seems particularly futile—"look, I don't know."

"Sure you do."

"I didn't tell them about you."

"Why not?"

"I don't know."

"Sure you do."

"Jesus Christ, Eden, stop telling me I know. Maybe I really don't know."

She looks at me, surprised. I realize how mean I sounded.

"I'm sorry."

"Again?" She sounds irritated. Impatient.

I look at her blankly.

"That's your second apology in two minutes after two months without any."

"Sorry," I say again.

"Okay, but I can't really know how I feel about it until you tell me why."

"You mean you can't forgive me until I tell you why."

"Right."

"Right," I echo.

I run my fingers through my hair and look at the ceiling. "Look, I just, I haven't been . . . I haven't been spending all that much time with them lately." It's the first time I've thought about it like that.

"With your parents?" Eden says.

"Right."

"On purpose?"

"Well, I spend so many nights at your place."

"I know. But you still spend plenty here."

"I know, I just, I don't spend time here with them."   •

"Well, I wouldn't say I 'spend time' with my parents," she says, "but they're there, at my house. I mean, they see what I do and where I'm going, and whatever. Unless I don't want them to."

She looks back at me now, and she sounds genuinely concerned, not angry. "Are you guys fighting? You're not talking to them?"

"No. I mean no, I'm not not talking to them."

"They're really nice, you know?"

"I know."

"So?"

"It has nothing to do with whether they're nice or not. Sure they're nice. They're the nicest people most people will ever meet." I take another step, but not toward her; I'm beginning to pace.

"I don't know. I didn't want to tell them about you."

"Why?" she says, and she sits back down on the bed, which makes me feel better.

"Because . . . I can't quite explain it," I say, and I sit down next to her, genuinely relieved to be close to her again. "Because this is mine—it's ours."

"Well, sure."

"But it's not theirs."

"You kept me a secret because this is our relationship not theirs? Or did you just forget to tell them about me?"

"I don't know—wait," I say, because I know she's exasperated with that answer. "I really don't. I'm trying to work this out."

"Okay," she says patiently, softly. "Work it out."

"I didn't forget to tell them about you. I thought about telling them about you. I just—I think I liked having a secret to keep from them."

"Why?"

I slouch beside her, look at the floor. "I told you, remember that time, I told you I was angry at them."

"Yeah?"

"I think I've been angry at them ever since then. But not like I wasn't talking to them or anything. It was more . . . more subtle than that. More like—I just thought it was my turn."

"Your turn for what?"

"My turn to have something that was a secret from them."

"Oh," she says, and she doesn't ask for any more of an answer, and I'm grateful. We study for about an hour, and then I walk her to the subway. I'd like to say it's out of chivalry, but it's really so we can make out on the corner above the subway station, since I still don't want to kiss her while my parents are home.

Thanksgiving

So, anyway, my parents are really into Thanksgiving. My mother cooks everything from scratch and my dad actually decorates. I once told him that I'd gotten old enough that the turkey balloons weren't necessary, and he said, "Don't flatter yourself, kiddo. We did this long before you came along."

"You did?"

"It's our favorite holiday," he said, as if that explained why a young couple would decorate their house with paper turkeys.

On Thanksgiving morning, my mom's already in the kitchen when I wake up. From my bedroom, I can hear her laying out ingredients for one of her two stuffing recipes.

"Morning, Nicky," she says, barely looking up from her cookbook when I walk into the room.

"Hey," I say, reaching for an apple.

"I'm really happy Eden will be able to join us this afternoon," she says. I shrug.

"She seems lovely," my mother tries. I shrug again and turn to head back to my room.

"Nick," she says to my back, and I stop and look over my shoulder. Having called my name, she seems lost. She looks down at her cookbook and turns the pages, as though the words she wants to say might be written down in there somewhere. Finally, she looks up and says, "Listen, I just want you to know that I'm here, if you want to talk about what's going on with your father. Or about Eden." She smiles. "Though I doubt you'd want to talk about that with me."

I almost smile back. But then I just shrug again and say, "Yeah, I doubt it, too." My mother turns back to her cookbook, and I head back to my room.

A few hours later, my dad is proudly showing me his latest Thanksgiving purchase: squash-shaped napkin rings.

"But we don't use cloth napkins."

"Why can't you put a paper napkin in a napkin ring?"

I shrug. "I don't know, I guess I never saw anyone do that."

"Well, I'm going to," he says. "Want to help?"

"Um. I'm gonna call Stevie. See what time he's coming over." I say this half to end the conversation, and half to answer his question: Stevie is always willing to help with the Thanksgiving decorations. As I retreat from the festivities to my room, it occurs to me that that was actually one of the longer conversations my father and I have had in the last few weeks. Or maybe months. I'm not keeping track.

He hasn't asked me about Eden once since they met her. Not that I would want to tell him anything. But he hasn't even asked.

Stevie's not picking up his cell phone, so I leave a message. "Dude, when are you gonna get here? Are you still sleeping? Call me back on the landline."

The phone rings two seconds later. "It's for me!" I call out, and answer it before either of them can pick up. I don't want them to hear me begging Stevie to come over early. It's strange, but I'm actually nervous being alone with my dad. I think it would help if Stevie were here to do the talking.

"Hey," I say, already pacing around my room.

"Hello."

I recognize the voice. "Hello," I say back. I've stopped pacing; now I'm perfectly still.

"You must be Nick; I'm Sam."

"Yeah, that's me."

"Happy Thanksgiving."

"Thanks. You too."

"Your dad says you guys put out quite a spread."

I start pacing again, circles this time, around the edge of my room. "Yeah, he loves Thanksgiving."

"Me too. My favorite holiday."

"Must be hereditary," I say, and I freeze in my steps as I say it, actually lifting my hand to my mouth, as though I can catch the words before they fall into the phone.

But Sam just laughs. "I guess it could be, huh?" He's cracking up, like really laughing hard.

"Dude," I say, "it's not really that funny."

"No, I guess it's not. Not to you."

Well, what the hell is that supposed to mean? Like there's some clandestine adoption humor I can't understand, but just accidentally tapped into?

"May I speak with Rob?" he says finally, still kind of laughing.

"Yeah, I'll get him," I say, and walk into the living room with the phone.

"Happy Thanksgiving," Sam says again as I walk toward my dad.

"Happy Thanksgiving," I mumble back, but I've already begun to hand over the phone, so I don't think he hears me. On the way back to my room, I hear Dad laughing. Maybe Sam told him what I said. And even though technically it's my joke, I feel left out.

I pick up my cell phone and call Stevie again. This time he picks up.

"Dude, stalker much?"

"When can you be here?"

"I just woke up."

"What do you mean you just woke up?"

"I understand it's a complicated concept. You see, Nicholas, at night the body does what is commonly known as sleeping, which is to say, enters a state of unconsciousness—"

"Shut up."

"You shut up."

"Will you come over now?"

"Can I shower first?"

"I really don't care."

"Dude, are you really this nervous about Eden coming to Thanksgiving?"

I'm grateful to hear that that's why he thinks I'm acting this way.

"Whatever, just get here ASAP."

"Did you just say ASAP?"

"No, of course not."

"Okay, then."

"Okay."

Thirty minutes later, and Stevie is standing in the kitchen, looking at my mother's turkey in the oven. His hair is still wet from the shower.

"Hey," I say, coming out of my bedroom, "I didn't hear you get here." The doormen never buzz him up, and my parents must have left the front door unlocked today. I'm not quite in the living room; I'm standing at the edge of the hallway that leads to our bedrooms. But from here I can see into the kitchen, which is just kind of an alcove off the living room. And I can see that Stevie looks more comfortable in our kitchen than I've been in a long time. My mom has her hand on Stevie's shoulder when he leans down to smell the turkey.

"It's going to be a good one this year," he says, smiling at her.

"It's always good," my dad says, watching them from the

dining room table. I don't know when he got off the phone. He's putting paper napkins into his new napkin rings. Stevie looks across the kitchen counter at the table.

"Dude, cool napkin rings, Rob. I call the zucchini!"

Well, lucky him, between Stevie and Sam Roth, my father has the perfect son now, one who appreciates his knickknacks and gets his jokes.

~⌒

Eden comes over around three. I told her that we don't dress up and also that she didn't have to bring anything, but she's wearing a skirt anyway and brings flowers for my mom. Stevie, Eden, and I sit on the couch, Eden in the middle. There's a football game on, but none of us is watching. My parents are in the kitchen, and we speak quietly, like little kids who've been told to keep it down.

"What kind of flowers are those?" Stevie says finally.

Eden raises her eyebrows at him. The flowers are roses. Even Stevie can see that.

"Sorry," Stevie says. "Just trying to break the tension."

"What tension?" I say quickly.

"Umm, have you noticed that you haven't said a word to your parents since I got here?" he says.

"That's not true."

"Yes it is."

Eden breaks in. "He said, 'I'll hang up Eden's coat.' "

"Quite the conversationalist you are this Thanksgiving day," Stevie says to me.

"Sorry. What would you like to talk about?"

Stevie perks up. "Let's talk about what your parents think of Eden."

Now Eden becomes alert.

"Did they say something to you?" she asks Stevie.

"Would you care if they did?" I ask sullenly, a sour taste in my mouth.

"Of course I would. Wouldn't you?"

"No," I say stubbornly. "Doesn't it only matter what *I* think of you?"

Stevie looks from me to Eden and back to me again.

"Dude, what is going on? Why are you so pissed at your parents? I was going to tell you how much they like Eden."

"They like me?" Eden says, smiling at Stevie.

I slump deeper into the couch, away from Eden and Stevie, who've begun to sit up straighter. "Seriously, Eden, why the hell do you care?" My mouth still tastes sour, like I'm a rotten apple and they're both still fresh and crisp.

Eden turns to face me.

"Seriously, Nick, why did you just talk to me like that? What is it that you are so pissed off about?"

I look at Stevie for support, but he shakes his head at me; even Stevie's not on my side here. I know I should explain why I'm being a total asshole.

I swallow. "Look, let's just have dinner first, okay?" I ask.

"First before what?" Stevie says.

"Just first. Please, okay?" I'm pleading. Stevie and Eden exchange a look, and I guess they must agree, because Stevie says, "Okay."

Dessert

We always take a break between dinner and dessert. Usually Stevie and I go back to my room for an hour or so, and my parents get out board games, and later we play while we eat pie and ice cream. All through dinner, I know Stevie's waiting for that hour, expecting that'll be when I'll explain the tension in the house, and that somehow my telling him will release all that tension so that he can enjoy his dessert. I also know Stevie feels bad for Eden. I know he wants to tell her that Thanksgiving at my house is usually a lot of fun. I know he wants to because I do, too.

I wonder if my parents think I've already told them about Sam Roth. I bet they think I've at least told Stevie.

Stevie shuts my bedroom door behind us.

"We waited," he says seriously.

"I know," I say, sliding down onto the floor and leaning back against the bed. Stevie sits on the floor across from me, leaning on my dresser. I expect Eden to sit down beside me, but instead she sits across from me with Stevie. I'm actually kind of grateful because that way I can look straight ahead at both of them while I tell them, even though I'm looking at the floor now.

I think maybe this will be a little less surprising for Eden. At least, she knows that I've been having issues with my parents for the last couple of months. I haven't said a word about it to Stevie. But then Stevie says, "Okay, I'll get this started. Something's been going on with you and your parents for the last couple months, right?"

I look straight at Stevie, and my surprise must be written on my face because he says, "Dude, it wasn't like you were hiding it or anything."

"I wasn't?"

Stevie gives me a look like Are you kidding?

"Okay, yeah. So I've been, you know, pissed at my parents for a couple months."

"At both of them?" Stevie asks.

I nod. "Yes." Then I shake my head slowly. "No. Yes, but mostly at my dad, really."

"Why?"

"I don't know."

"Look, dude," Stevie says, "you don't have to tell us, or me, anything you don't want to, but don't lie. Something must have happened to jump-start all this, right?"

"Yes. Right."

"You don't have to tell us if you don't want to," Eden echoes.

"I don't want to," I say.

Stevie grins. "Well, fuck it, man, I was lying, you gotta tell us."

"No he doesn't," Eden says, punching Stevie in the arm.

"Yes I do," I say finally. "I'm not being—I haven't been nice since all this started."

"You're nice to me," Eden says.

Stevie shushes her. "Let him say it."

"You're just curious," Eden says.

"Do I have to be here for this conversation?" I ask.

They both say "sorry" and I smile at them. The past couple of months should have been perfect. I've been falling in love with this girl who is so amazing she can actually go nine rounds of verbal boxing with Stevie and come out on top from time to time. This makes me very, very angry at my dad. Like he's stolen two perfect months from me, made it so that they weren't perfect, two months I will never get back again.

So I tell them. I tell them that when my dad was in college he had a girlfriend back home, but I don't tell them her name was Sarah Booker. I tell them that there was a phone call, but I don't tell them about my theory that maybe some guy was trying to extort money from my father. I tell them there was a baby who grew up in Texas and now he's getting married. I tell them my father's been on the registry for eleven years, but I don't tell them about the temper tantrum I had when I found that out.

Then I turn to Eden and say, "I told you my parents weren't perfect."

Eden slides across the floor to sit next to me, and holds my hand. She helped my mother with the apple pie before, and now she smells like cinnamon. It's so comforting that I breathe a little deeper. I start to relax a little.

But then Stevie says, "What the fuck do you sound so bitter for?"

"What's that supposed to mean?"

"This is something that happened to your dad, not to you."

"Of course it's something that happened to me." I drop Eden's hand and look straight at Stevie.

"It's your dad's bad luck, not yours."

"Bad luck?" I repeat, the words sounding small. Something like this can't possibly be boiled down to two simple syllables.

"That's all this is: your dad had bad luck. Nicholas, we're all going to have stupid sex at some point—sex without protection, secret sex, drunken sex, sex with the wrong person, sex for the wrong reasons. And you know what we'll be doing while we have this stupid sex?"

"I imagine we'll be having sex," I say snarkily.

Stevie glares at me. "We'll all just close our eyes and hope for the best. We'll hope that we'll be lucky." Stevie's face softens. "Your dad just had the unlucky kind of sex."

"Or the lucky kind," Eden says, and Stevie and I both look at her like she's crazy.

"It was good luck for someone," she continues. "Someone must have wanted Sam very much."

Stevie nods. "See, it was just luck," he says. "Good or bad."

"Seems like a lot of trouble for just a little bit of luck, huh?" I say, angry that they can't see that everything has changed.

"Or maybe not so much trouble," Stevie says. "I mean, does this seem like that much trouble to your parents?"

"I don't know."

"Well, how could you when you're barely talking to them?" Stevie says. And Eden nods.

I look at Stevie. "It's not my fault I'm barely talking to them."

"How do you figure that?" Stevie asks.

"They started it."

Stevie grins at me. "All right, kindergarten boy."

"But they did. My dad started the silence when he decided not to talk to me about this years ago. And my mom kept it going when she agreed to go along with his decision."

I'm looking at Stevie, but he's looking at Eden, and Eden's look must be telling him to drop it, because Stevie is quiet for a second, like he's trying to work something out. He must decide it's not worth arguing about, because he says, "Hey, know what I just thought of?"

"What?"

"You're the only one of us who's not an only child now."

"I guess that's true, huh?" Eden says.

"I don't get it," I say.

Eden takes my hand and squeezes, tight. "Plenty of people

get surprised with a new baby brother. A new big brother is something different altogether."

"I can't believe you're dating someone who says 'altogether,'" Stevie says, and I smile, though mostly I'm hearing what Eden said. It hadn't actually occurred to me, really, that Sam was my brother.

"Dessert will be ready," I say, finally.

"Sweet," Stevie says, peeling himself off the floor.

"Literally," Eden and I say in unison, and Stevie rolls his eyes.

"Please don't become that couple," he says.

I open the door to my bedroom. Eden walks out first, and then Stevie, but he stops and turns to me and says, "It's like suddenly having sibling rivalry after sixteen years of having your dad all to yourself."

"Go eat your pie," I say, pushing him into the hallway. I don't have the energy to be mad at Stevie and my parents at the same time.

The Bad Dream

I dreamed about Eden last night. In my dream, she broke up with me. We were sitting on a bench and she told me that this had all gotten too complicated, and her hair fell into her face, but it wasn't really her hair, it was blonder, kind of see-through, because even though it was covering her face, I could see her eyes and she wasn't crying at all.

"What's too complicated?"

"It's not what I thought it would be," she said.

"What did you think it would be?"

"I thought it would be perfect. Like they were."

In the dream, she meant my parents. She meant my family.

She didn't want me anymore because my parents weren't perfect, because we weren't so different from her family after all. And when I woke up, I knew it was true. And I hated my parents for it. So now, even though it's the day after Thanksgiving, and I don't have any homework, I'm holed up in my room studying, because it's keeping me busy. Way too busy to go out there, and way too busy for them to come in here.

Except for then my dad knocks on the door.

"Hey."

I look at him. I'm still in bed. And okay, maybe I wasn't studying so much as staring up at the ceiling with some books in my lap, trying to figure out how I could salvage my relationship with Eden, the girl who never smells the same but whose every scent feels like home.

"Hey," I say back.

"Studying?"

I look down at my books. Isn't it obvious?

"Feel like some leftovers?"

"No," I say, and even I'm surprised at how abrupt it sounds.

He's only halfway through the door, which is still only halfway open. He seems scared to come in.

"Listen, Dad, if that's all, then I really have to study now."

Then he surprises me by opening the door wide and stepping inside, all the way, and without hesitating he walks straight to my bed. He sits down and faces me.

"No, that's not all, as a matter of fact."

"What else could there possibly be? A secret daughter this time, holed up in West Virginia?"

I expect that to shut him up, but instead he smiles and says, "Why West Virginia?"

"Had to think of a state that would be worse than Texas," I say meanly.

"Jesus Christ, Nick, when did you get so damned snotty?"

"Snotty?" I repeat angrily. What the hell? My father, the man who doesn't even yell at boys stealing bicycles, has the audacity to yell at me because he doesn't like the way I've responded to his secret-love-child-ridden past.

"Superior, like that. Like somehow you're better than me, or than Sam, because you're from New York, and things like that don't happen to people here—do you really believe that? That no one in New York makes mistakes, that up here you all know better than us Midwestern-Southern know-nothings?"

I answer too fast, before I even know what I'm about to say.

"Maybe, because I don't know anyone who's not smart enough to use birth control."

A normal father would hit me for saying something like that. A normal father would get off the bed, yell at me, slam the door behind him. But my father sits there. He looks crushed. He looks disappointed, not in me, but in himself, that he could have raised a son who would say something so mean.

"Well," he says finally, "I hope you're right. Because I would hate to be your friend if I'd screwed up: I would hate to have to come to you for any kind of help or understanding."

I don't say anything. Dad gets up off the bed and takes a couple of steps toward the door.

"In any case, I was just coming in here to tell you that Sam's coming to Ohio for Christmas with us."

"What?"

"He wants to see where he's from. He wants to meet me."

"What are you going to tell everyone?"

"I'd been planning on asking you your opinion, but I don't think I will now." He says that like it's a punishment to me, for him not to want my advice.

He closes the door behind him, and I realize that it actually is a terrible punishment: my opinion doesn't hold weight anymore.

Perfection on Black Friday

I never believed in going places without calling first. There's no excuse anymore—everyone has cell phones and BlackBerrys, text messages and email. But I need to get out of the house, and I don't feel like calling. So thirty minutes later I'm in Eden's lobby, pressing the intercom so that she'll let me up.

"What are you doing here?" Jesus Christ, was she always this beautiful? The way Eden looks is a constant source of fascination to me. I would never call her pretty. Pretty girls are simpler; their hair isn't so thick and their lips aren't so dark. Pretty girls smile easily and often; Eden's smiles are rewarding.

"Are your parents home?" I ask.

"No."

"Okay."

"What are you doing here?" she repeats.

I shrug.

"I mean, of course you're welcome. You just usually call."

"I'm sorry."

"I don't mind. I'm happy you're here. I wanted to talk to you."

Oh God. She wanted to talk to me. That's what people say when they want to break up with you. She's going to take her freckled skin and her brown hair as far as she can from all this melodrama.

"Can we just sit down?" I say desperately, looking around the living room for a place to land.

"Of course we can sit down," she says, like it's no big deal. No big deal, she's just dumping me. She turns her back on me and walks to her room, and I walk slowly behind her. Her hair is in a ponytail but pieces of it have fallen out of the elastic, trailing down her back. She's wearing a tank top and I can see her shoulders, white and shining, like they've never seen the sun, her shoulder blades jutting through like wings.

Apparently, I wax poetic when I'm about to be dumped.

Eden closes the door to her room, and I sit on the floor, leaning my back against the bed.

"I dreamed about this last night," I say.

"Dreamed about what?"

"This conversation. But we weren't in your room. We were on a bench."

"Where?" Eden is standing over me. I usually feel so tall when I'm with her, so much more like a man. But now I feel small, a little boy waiting for his punishment.

I shrug. "Not sure. The park, maybe."

"Oh." She nods, and then she says, "So, how are you? Did you and your parents talk at all after we left?" She sits now, but not right next to me. She's out of my reach.

I press into my cheeks with both hands. "You don't have to do that."

"Do what?"

"Ask about my parents. I know you didn't want any of that."

"Any of what?"

"It's not what you wanted to get into, I know that."

"Well, I'm glad one of us knows something, because I have no idea what you're talking about."

"You liked my family."

"I still like your family."

I laugh, "Yeah, like this was the family you had in mind."

"Nick, you're not making any sense. Seriously." She slides across the floor, closer to me. She takes my hand and holds it in her lap. Her skin is cool and soft.

"That's like when you showed me how my parents held hands."

"You wanted to kiss me then, didn't you?"

I smile. "Sure I did."

"Well, you can now."

I shake my head. "No, I can't."

"Why not?"

"It would just make this last longer."

"Make what last longer?"

"Listen, let's get it over with, okay? I know you don't want me anymore."

"I don't?"

I shake my head. "Everything's a mess."

"Not everything. Many things are still neat and clean and exactly where they're supposed to be."

"Like what?"

"Like you and me, sitting on the floor of my room."

"But you didn't sign up for this. You liked how perfect everything was—how perfect my family was."

"Well, sure I did. Normal is exotic to me. But, Nick, that's not why I like you."

I don't look at her.

"Seriously, Nick, is that really what you thought? That I wanted to be with you because your family was so neat when mine was so messy?"

I look at our hands in her lap. Her skin is so much paler than mine.

"Nick, I don't love you because of your family. I love you because I just love you."

And slowly I raise my head to look at her. She's looking straight at me. She's *smiling* at me. And she loves me.

Holy shit, she loves me. She's not breaking up with me—she wanted to tell me that she loves me. Whew, did I misread the signals! Fucking idiot.

Wait, why has she stopped smiling? Why is she raising her

eyebrows at me like there's something I've done wrong now, something I forgot to do, like how my mom looks at my dad when he forgets to put the toilet seat down? All she has to do is come into the living room with that look on her face and Dad knows what he's done.

Crap. This is some big, important moment, and I've just done the verbal equivalent of leaving the toilet seat up.

"Oh. Oh, of course. I thought you knew. I love you, too."

"But you're supposed to say it, you idiot," she says, shoving me. I fall back onto the carpet, taking her down with me.

"I love you, too," I say again, quieter now, with my hands on either side of her face, and I kiss her, probably softer than I've ever kissed anyone before, and I feel so safe, because we love each other now, so this isn't ending. Fuck it, I'm gonna just say the cheesiest thing I can think of: It's not the end, it's the beginning.

And we don't stop kissing, and I know something else. I know we're going to have sex. Right now, on her floor, the day after Thanksgiving. I've never wanted anything like I want Eden now. Nothing we've done has been like this. None of our kisses have ever felt like this. And her skin has never been so soft, and it's never been so natural to slide her pants off, to kick my shoes off, to take her hair out of its ponytail and watch it fall around her face.

We stop for a second. I remember that I have condoms in my jeans pockets, left over from that day when Stevie shoved them in my backpack. After Eden and I became a real couple, I optimistically moved a few of them from my backpack to my jeans, just in case. And I haven't even washed the jeans since. They're months old, but condoms don't expire after just a few months, right?

And when I'm almost inside her, suddenly that's all I'm thinking about. They're still good, right? They're still working. Condoms don't go bad in a matter of months. I should have looked at the expiration date first. I know better than that. I'm smarter than that.

Expiration date, expiration date. It's all I can think. How is that what I'm thinking about now? Why is that what I'm thinking about now? But there it is again: Expiration date. Expiration date. When I close my eyes, all I see is the wrapper before I ripped it, but the date is too blurry to make out.

But then Eden's arms squeeze my neck, and my body relaxes over hers, and then I can't hold another thought in my head. The only thing I can feel is Eden. I can't feel the end of the desk against which my foot is lodged and I can't feel my belt discarded underneath my knee. I don't feel the carpet scratching my hands and I will have to think, later, to remember why my hands are so red. The only thing I'm aware of is Eden and her arms around my neck and her legs touching mine and her skin under my hands. Nothing, I think, has ever felt this good. And maybe no one in the world has ever been so perfectly in love.

I won't think about the expiration date again until much later. When I'm at home and I look at my dad, and I wonder what he was thinking about when he was with Sarah Booker.

Invitations

 E den and I didn't really talk much after. Actually, she started
laughing almost as soon as we finished, giggling—something she
does so rarely—and in a few minutes I was laughing, too. Apparently, we both thought that having had sex with each other was
hilarious. But then we heard her mother getting off the elevator, so we got dressed, and stopped laughing, and then I left, and
now I'm almost home. I'll call her in a little while; I already miss
her. When Stevie finds out, he'll joke that I'm like one of those
guys who only say "I love you" to bed some girl. I start laughing
again as I open our front door. But then I see my dad sitting on
the couch, and I can't remember what was ever so funny to me.

Now I remember that Sam is coming at Christmas. I never got around to telling Eden that.

"Hey, Buddy," my dad says as I walk across the living room. My plan had been to go straight to my room, but now I can't remember the last time he called me Buddy, even if it was a nickname I was trying to outgrow. I'm not sure if we're angry at each other anymore.

I hesitate before answering. I have no idea how to hang out with my dad anymore. I honestly don't remember how to do it.

"Hey, Buddy," I say back, finally. I've stopped in the middle of the room. "Eating leftovers?" He's got a Tupperware full of stuffing on his lap. He holds it out to me, and I know it's really an invitation to sit down.

"Stuffing as peace offering," I say, grabbing his fork and sitting down next to him.

I wonder whose idea it was. Like Sam probably said that he wanted to meet my dad. Or maybe he said that he wanted to see where he was born. But who suggested he come at Christmastime?

"Whose idea was it?"

"Which one?"

"Which one?" I repeat.

"That we give Sam up for adoption? That Mom use fennel instead of cloves in the stuffing this year? That Sam come for Christmas?"

"That one. The last one."

Dad leans back now, sinking into the couch. I'm still perched on the edge with the stuffing and the fork.

"I don't remember."

"You're lying."

Even though he's behind me, I can tell he's shaking his head.

"I don't remember whose idea it was that we meet. But yes, I invited him."

"Don't you think you should have asked us first—your parents, or Mom, or me?"

"Your mother thought I should have. She was pretty angry I didn't talk to you about it first, actually."

Good for Mom, I think.

"But it didn't happen like that," Dad continues. "It just seemed so natural to invite him. I couldn't help it."

"I see."

"Do you?" he says, and I turn to face him. He looks tired but I don't feel sorry for him.

"Didn't his parents care that he'd miss Christmas?"

Dad shakes his head. "No—they're Jewish."

"So am I, technically."

"Well, they're the kind of Jews who don't do Christmas. His fiancée's Catholic, I think, so he usually spends Christmas with them. But I guess they said it was okay that he miss it this year."

I kind of wish Sam didn't have such an understanding fiancée.

"When's he getting married?" I ask.

"In the spring—April."

"Are you invited to his wedding?"

Dad looks surprised. "Of course not."

"Why not?"

"We hardly know each other yet."

They hardly know each other. Yet.

"Do the people who adopted him know he's been talking to you?"

"He hasn't told me whether he's said anything to his parents."

"You sure are a fount of information."

Dad grins. I think he's proud of me for using the word "fount."

"Well, it seems to me you should be invited to his wedding. You invited him to Christmas."

"I'm not sure that's a fair exchange of invitations."

"What are you going to tell people about him?"

Dad shrugs. "I don't know. The truth, I guess. I'm not ashamed of it anymore."

"You're not?"

Dad sits up, puts his face close to mine.

"I can't be ashamed to be attached to Sam, now that I know him."

"You said you hardly knew him."

"You're right, that's true."

"You sure have a fuzzy idea of truth right now. You don't remember whose idea it was for him to come at Christmas, but you invited him. You hardly know him, but you know that he's so great that you're proud to know him, too."

"Sometimes the truth is like that, I guess."

"I thought that truth was an absolute."

"In theory, maybe. In practice, I'm finding that it's much more . . . I don't know. It's shifting."

Now I lean back, too, next to him. "Like a few months ago it was true that I was your only son." It's the first time I've ever called Sam his son. The word leaves a heavy taste in my mouth after I've said it. "That's some shift," I say.

"Sam is really someone else's son."

"But he's yours, too."

"Only sort of."

"You sure have become a lot more vague since Sam came into our lives."

"Nick, he was always in my life."

Does he realize how creepy that sounds? Like Sam was some kind of specter, haunting us for the past thirty years. Just because he and Sarah Booker couldn't keep their pants on. Or didn't use birth control. Or used an expired condom.

Dad gets up now. "You want me to put the stuffing back in the fridge, or are you still working on it?"

"No, you can take it," I say.

"Nick?" he says, like my name itself is a question.

"I don't want to talk about it anymore," I say sullenly. I feel like a bratty little kid; it wasn't that long ago I felt like a grown-up in love.

"Okay," he says, and I get up to go to my room.

"Hey, Dad." I look toward the kitchen. His back is to me; he's leaning over into the fridge. I ask quickly, before he turns around: "Did you love Sarah—was she your first love?"

Dad turns and he doesn't answer until his eyes are looking straight at me.

"She was my first everything," he says earnestly. His face looks like something from the movies, or from those shows on channel eleven about teenagers in love.

I can only imagine mine looks like that when I think about Eden.

The True Meaning
of Christmas

I've been home for two hours and I haven't called Eden yet. But I will call her. I plan to call her.

It's dark out already. People are brushing their teeth, changing into their pajamas, watching Christmas specials, because now that it's Thanksgiving, Christmas is just around the corner.

Oh Christ, Christmas is coming.

There must be some kind of metaphor to be made here, something about the son from a mysterious conception appearing at Christmastime. Someone would say something about Troy being the name of an ancient city. Although it's the wrong city, in the wrong part of the world for this story.

Actually, I guess Christmas has plenty of meaning for me. I mean, we have traditions. We do the tree thing and presents and stockings and go shopping like Americans should. We have traditions, and none of them have to do with this mysterious son showing up and changing everything.

Jesus, when did my life turn into some after-school Christmas movie-of-the-week special? With B-list former-child-star actors. I wonder who'd play me. I wonder who'd play Sam, since I have no idea what the eff he looks like.

And then what he looks like is all I can think about. Having no idea what Sarah Booker looked like, I can only imagine what features he may have gotten from my dad. Gray eyes, maybe, or a dimple in his chin. I have my dad's mouth; maybe Sam has it, too.

And now I'm really fucking pissed off that some guy is walking around Texas wearing my fucking mouth. I purse my lips. I actually go over to the mirror on the back of my door and take stock. What features could I have in common with Sam Roth: I have my dad's mouth. I have my dad's hair. I have my dad's hands and his small feet, even though I'm tall like my mom. See, Sam couldn't have that, he couldn't have my small feet/height combination because that is unique to my parents' coupling.

But what if Sarah Booker was tall, too? What if—and I can't believe I'm considering this—that's my dad's type? Maybe Sarah Booker looked like my mother.

And then I remember something. My dad's high school yearbooks are in the living room, on a shelf next to the TV. He brought them from my grandparents' house a few years ago, when they decided it was time to move to a smaller place. But my dad is in the living room, and he'll know exactly what I'm up to if he sees me looking at his yearbook. I have to wait until they're asleep.

And so I wait. I wait until my mom peeks her head in the door to tell me good night, until I hear the clicks of lights being switched off, toilets being flushed; I imagine I can even hear their breathing getting slower, even though they're all the way down the hall. I wait until I can't even hear the people on the floor above us moving around anymore, as though if they were awake to hear me, they could somehow alert my parents.

It's near midnight when I walk into the living room. I turn on only my dad's small desk lamp. The yearbooks are on a high shelf, as though my dad never intended to look at them. And certainly never intended for me to look at them.

It's easy to find my dad's yearbook page. I used to look through his yearbooks when I was little, at my grandparents' house. It's been years, but I remember the picture right away. He really doesn't look much different now than he did in high school. He's thinner now, maybe; his jaw juts out more. Maybe he still had baby fat then, which I guess means that maybe I still have baby fat, since I'm a year younger now than he was when he took his senior yearbook picture. I'm looking so closely at my dad that it takes me a second to notice that the name on the picture directly to the left of his is Sarah Booker.

Of course. I should have expected that. Brandt coming right after Booker. I bet they liked that; I'd want my picture next to

Eden's in something official like a yearbook. I give myself a min-ute before I look up at the picture above the name. It's funny because no doubt I've actually seen it before, when I was little, looking over all the pictures. Maybe I even asked my dad which girl was his girlfriend. Maybe he even pointed her out to me.

She's blond. The picture's in black and white, but you can still tell. Blond, and there are freckles across her nose, and her face is very round. Her mouth is open wide in a smile and there is a gap between her two front teeth, which are very straight and very white. She almost looks like she's laughing.

She looks nothing like my mother, whose hair is dark and whose skin is very white, and who usually smiles with her mouth only slightly open. Either my dad doesn't have a type or his type changed when he met my mother.

I close the yearbook. What had I expected—that I'd look at the picture and suddenly know exactly what Sam looks like? You could hardly look at a picture of my parents—of anyone's parents—and be able to know what their child looked like.

Sarah Booker is very pretty, I think as I stand on my toes to put the book back on its shelf, careful to put it back in between the same two books I'd taken it out from. She's very pretty; my dad was probably very proud to have had such a pretty girlfriend. I bet he stood up a little straighter when they walked down the street. I know, because I do that when I walk with Eden.

I try to picture my father as a teenager in love; it surprises me that it's difficult. I never knew I was the type of son who sees his father as nothing other than a father. I never considered that he'd been young and loved someone before my mother.

Come to think of it, I never much considered his love for my mother beyond its making a marriage and making me. But every father has had a past, not just mine; and so I shouldn't have been so surprised to find out about it, even if it is manifesting itself in a living, breathing thirty-year-old man instead of maybe some black-and-white photos in an attic or an old joint in his childhood bedroom. I think of how quickly I dismissed it, after Simon Natherton's party, when my dad told me that he'd gotten drunk on a rooftop, just like I had. It's like how you never imagine your teachers outside of school, and of course, they have other lives.

I switch off the light on my father's desk and head back to my room. I nearly shout when I stub my toe on the coffee table. I know this room so well, but I'm still such a klutz. Just like my dad, actually. My mom always says I would have been luckier to inherit her coordination.

I didn't even leave any of the lights on in my room. I was pretending that I'd gone to sleep, too. I limp toward my bed, cursing my toe for having the gall to walk into the coffee table. Or maybe I should be cursing the coffee table. I slide beneath the covers, pulling them up all the way over my head, trying not to see Sarah Booker's blond-girl face when I close my eyes. I'm suddenly very, very tired, and very, very happy to be in my bed.

Oh shit, I never called Eden.

The Morning After

I wake up early. I wish I were a runner. I've never gone running, but this morning I wish I were the kind of person who'd go out in the brisk November air and run this early, the time of day that only cab drivers and doormen and runners know well. But I'm not the kind of person who goes for a run when he wakes up early. I'm the kind of person who stays in bed and stares at the ceiling.

It's too early to do anything. It's too early to watch TV; nothing's on at this hour. It's too early to eat Thanksgiving leftovers. And it's too early to call Eden.

I forgot to call Eden. And I'm surprised by it, surprised that

I barely thought about her last night; for the last few months, every time I was doing something else, I was thinking about being with Eden instead. But I don't remember thinking about anything except for whether or not Sam was walking around Texas with a face that looked like mine.

It's even too early for my parents to be awake, for my mom to be walking Pilot, so I'm surprised when I hear someone moving around outside my room. It's not Mom and Pilot, because I don't hear Pilot's paws clicking on the hardwood. It's shuffling, like someone who's trying to keep his slippers from falling off. I know it's my dad, and I get out of bed.

When I walk into the living room, I get an idea of what I must have looked like last night. He's only turned on his desk lamp, and he's standing on his toes reaching for his high school yearbook.

"Hey, Dad," I say softly. He looks so small that I'm worried he'll fall if I startle him.

Once he's grabbed his yearbook, he turns around and sees me.

"Hey, Buddy," he says, "you're up early."

"Yeah, well."

"Couldn't sleep?"

"Just couldn't sleep late."

He smiles. "Me too, I guess."

I wonder why he's getting the yearbook down now. I wonder if he can tell that I looked through it last night. I look at it in his hands, trying to figure out what could give me away. He notices me staring.

"Oh, this," he says. "Just feeling a little nostalgic, I guess."

I don't know what to say. Nostalgia seems like a strange emotion to be having when the child you gave up for adoption resurfaces. I mean, I can understand it might make you think about the past, but nostalgia doesn't seem like the right word. Maybe I'll look it up later. Maybe it has other meanings I don't know about.

But then he surprises me by saying, "You and Eden, at Thanksgiving. I know it must make me sound like your old, old dad, but it got me thinking about Sarah, you know. The high school girlfriend."

Something about the way he's summed her up makes me uneasy; we're still dating and in my dad's mind she's already just a fond memory.

"She's not just a high school girlfriend," I say, thinking about everything that happened yesterday.

"I didn't mean it like that. I just meant . . . I don't know. You never love anyone again the way you love your high school girl-friend. I can't explain it. I love your mother more than anything, but it's so different from what I felt for Sarah. Maybe it's because Sarah was the first person I'd ever been in love with. Maybe when an emotion is new, it's like you're testing it out, check-ing to see what the boundaries of it are. And later you can feel it even more, even better, even stronger, but . . ." He pauses, like he's looking for the right words. Finally, he says, "But it'll never feel that fresh again. And that makes it so intense."

I think about that. Does that mean what he felt for Sam,

when he was born, is more intense than what he felt for me, when I was?

"Anyway. I just felt like reading what she wrote in my year-book. I don't even remember it now."

"Oh. Okay." I'm still standing at the edge of the living room. He's still standing next to the bookshelves. Neither of us moves.

"Do you"—he hesitates—"would you like to see her picture?" He says it shyly; I think he's actually nervous to be talking to me, treading carefully because he doesn't know what'll set me off.

He says, "I thought you might be curious."

"If I were curious, I could have looked before," I say. The idea is so obvious, even if I didn't think of it myself until last night.

"Yeah, I guess you could have." He sits down on the couch now, the yearbook on his lap.

I go to sit next to him. "I'll look," I say, and he smiles. Through the couch cushions, I can actually feel him relaxing. And so I sit with him, and I look at Sarah's pictures. There's more than I saw last night. There are pictures of her as a cheerleader, and there's the note she left in the back of the book, which my father lets me read. She tells him that she loves him, and how much she'll miss him when he goes away to college, and it's clear that neither of them thought that the relationship was going to end just because he was going away. And it didn't, I guess, for a few years.

And soon it's late enough that I guess I could call Eden. She'd definitely be awake now, I think, every time I look up and see the clock on the cable box. But I don't get up. I sit there with my dad, and then we move to the dining room table and we eat leftovers. I sneak some food to Pilot when Dad's not looking. We watch football and I'm almost comfortable, sitting next to him, or anyway, less uncomfortable than I have been near him in a long time.

And I don't call Eden until much, much later.

Much, Much Later

It's nine o'clock that night when I call Eden. I'm sitting on the edge of my bed.

"Hey."

"Hi." There's silence, like Eden's waiting for more from me than "Hi." I know she thinks I should explain why I haven't called. But instead I say, "What are you up to?"

"I've been waiting for your call."

I laugh, but it comes out like a cackle.

"Aren't girls supposed to lie about things like that?" I ask.

"Like what?"

"Like, aren't you supposed to tell me how busy you've been, so busy that you haven't even noticed that I didn't call?"

"No. That would give you a free pass for not having called."

"But guys are supposed to be flaky about that." I'm lying; I know it's a big deal that I haven't called. I know I'm an asshole for not having called. I shouldn't make her feel like she's wrong to think it's important.

"Not the guy I'm dating."

"Are you dating someone else I should know about?" I say; I mean for it to be a joke, but it's not. It's mean.

"Well, I was dating this nice guy who never forgot to call and certainly never stood me up."

"I didn't stand you up," I say, but as soon as I say it, I remember that it's true. We were supposed to go to the movies today.

"I forgot about the movies," I say, but then I add, "but you could have called me to remind me."

Eden doesn't say anything for a second. But then she surprises me by saying, "You're right, I could have called you."

"I'm right?" I repeat, genuinely surprised.

"Look, Nick, you should have called. You definitely should have called. But I should have called, too."

"Right," I say, still not fully understanding, but happy to go along with any conversation that makes me right. But I still press my feet onto the floor and tense the muscles in my legs, just in case I need to be ready to spring to my own defense.

"Look, it was a big thing that happened. Huge. But maybe . . ." I can tell she's chewing her lip, thinking hard. "It was big for both of us, but maybe it was big for you in another way, a way that doesn't apply to me."

I want to make a joke about her using the word "big" again and again.

But I say, "I don't understand what you mean."

"I mean, you just found out that adolescent sex got your father into . . . let's call it trouble. And so maybe you were dealing with some heavy stuff that I can't relate to."

"It wasn't adolescent sex," I say.

"What?"

"He was in his twenties. So it wasn't adolescent."

I can see her nodding, considering her miscalculation. I can see that she is sitting on the edge of her bed, perched carefully, just like she's trying to choose her words carefully.

"Sure. But still," she says, and her voice is genuinely sweet. When I respond, my voice is genuinely nasty. I know I sound condescending.

"No, but still. It's totally different. One thing has nothing to do with the other." I press my feet harder into the floor and stand up. I'm doubly an asshole; here she is making excuses for me, for my not calling her, and here I am, giving her a hard time about it.

"Nick, I'm trying to be sensitive here. To say nothing of the fact that I'm giving you a free pass after we slept together and you didn't call. Like some cliché out of a bad movie."

"Oh, I'm sorry it was such a typical experience for you."

"Would you stop it? What is the matter with you?"

What *is* the matter with me? I take a step away from the bed. I actually drop the phone from my ear, let my arms hang down at my sides, and let my head fall back so that I'm looking at the ceiling. I lift the phone back up.

"Are you there?" Eden says.

"I'm here." I wish I still had the condom wrapper. I contemplate asking her to fish it out of the garbage. I left it on the floor, but I can picture her picking it up and putting it into the wicker wastebasket under her desk.

"And?" Eden prompts.

"And what?"

"And you're sorry!" she supplies for me. "Jeez Louise, I can't pick the words for you on top of everything else."

"What everything else?"

"Being the one to explain why you didn't call."

I want to tell her she's wrong. She doesn't know or understand why I didn't call. I don't know or understand why I didn't call. But I'm tired, so I say, "I *am* sorry, Eden." And I am, even if I'm not sure what for. But this seems to be enough.

"I know."

"Okay?"

"Yes, Nick, we're okay."

"Okay," I repeat, and I walk back over to my bed and sit back down. It doesn't feel like we're okay to me. But I decide to ignore it; I'll wait and see how it feels when I next see her. So I smile and say, "Hey, lady, did you just say 'Jeez Louise'?"

"Of course not," Eden says quickly.

"No, I think you did. I think you said 'Jeez Louise.' "

"It must have been someone else."

I lean back now, onto the pillows, relaxing. I imagine Eden is doing the same thing, her hair fanning out on her white bedspread.

"Must've been," I echo.

How to Completely Blow Everything with the Girl of Your Dreams

A Step-by-Step Guide, by Nicholas Brandt

Step 1: Fall in Love

Pine over her for the better part of middle school and high school. Finally work up the nerve to kiss her. Spend an amazing few months together. Find out what her favorite color is, take her to her favorite restaurants, learn where she's ticklish, how she likes to be kissed, and that the back of her neck always smells inexplicably like yellow-cake batter.

Tell her you love her.

Step 2: Physical Expression of Said Love

Have sex with her. Warning: It will be perfect. It will be everything the storybooks said it would be: fireworks, lightning bolts, eyes closed, mouth open. Memorize all of the freckles sprinkled over her torso, especially that dark brown one between her breasts.

Step 3: Neuroticism

Obsess over the expiration date of the condom you used, even though you know that the school nurse replenishes her condoms every month and they've only been in your pockets for two months, so they can't be more than three months old. Curse the nurse for being too cheap to get brand-name condoms.

Step 4: Be an Ass

Wait more than twenty-four hours following said sex before calling her.

Step 5: Be a Bigger Ass

Don't apologize for taking so long to call her; wait until she gives you the words to say. In fact, let her say all the right things for you. And don't repeat "I love you." Decide you're that kind of tough guy who only needs to say it once, even though over the previous sixteen years, you haven't exhibited one ounce of tough-guyness.

Step 6: Everything Feels Different (Even if It's Only in Your Head)

When you see her in school on Monday, act totally normal even though everything feels different. You can't put your finger on it, but being around her will feel itchy when before it would make your skin feel cool all over. You would do anything to make the itch go away, so you pretend you don't hear her when she asks what you're up to after school.

When your best friend asks you what's up your butt, say:

"Nothing, nothing. What could you possibly mean? Nothing."

"That's a lot of nothings for a whole bunch of something."

"Don't be a smart-ass."

"Don't be a jackass."

"You're my friend, not hers, aren't you?"

"What the fuck is that supposed to mean?"

"You know exactly what it means. Now let's get to class."

Step 7: Betrayal

In order to insure that you're becoming emotionally distant, withhold a significant piece of information about something significant that's going on in your life. For example, don't tell her that Sam is coming at Christmas. Then when she finds out through other means, she'll feel humiliated, hurt, and betrayed.

Here is a sample scenario to illustrate this all-important step:

One day after school my father is checking his email and

smiling. Eden and I are sitting on the couch, but when Eden gets up for some water, she turns and sees my dad's smile.

"What's got you so happy, Rob?" Eden asks.

"This? It's a note from my friend Sam." My father has developed the annoying habit of referring to Sam as his "friend." "He was asking what kind of clothes he needs for Ohio the week after next. For Christmas."

Eden looks at me, frozen between the couch and the kitchen. She looks confused. This must be some other Sam, her face says; Nick would have told me if it was *that* Sam. But I don't say anything, and I know she would never ask me in front of my dad. And I make sure we're not alone for the rest of the evening; we stay in the living room with my dad, and even when she leaves, I say good-bye at the doorway, where my father can still see us.

Step 8: Communication Is Key

Now this one is really very important: Don't have sex with her again. I know, this sounds physically impossible for a healthy, active adolescent boy. But it can be done. Wait until you're alone—and make sure that's not until at least a week has passed since you had sex the first time—and when she kisses you, all your muscles will clench. Believe me; her kisses will actually turn you off. And then she'll stop and ask:

"What's wrong?"

"Nothing."

"You're lying."

I lean my head back against her bed. We're on the floor of her room again. I look down at her carpet.

"I remember the first time I came over here."

"Me too," she says quietly. She is sitting crossed-legged, facing me.

"I was excited just to be in your room. I was so curious to see what it looked like, what was on your walls, whether your bed would be up against the wall or in the middle of the room, what street your window looked out on."

"And now?" she asks.

"Now I can see it all with my eyes closed. Now I don't have to wonder." There is something strange in my voice; it sounds like I miss wondering.

"Nick, seriously, talk to me. What's wrong?"

"Seriously talk to you?"

"You're not funny, Nick. You haven't been the same since last week."

I sit up. "Well, everything changed last week. Nothing is the same anymore."

Eden sits up and faces me. "Many things are the same. My room is the same: that my bed is in the middle of the room is the same, that my window looks out onto Duane Street is the same. That my walls are painted green is the same."

I look at the walls above us. "You call this green? I think it's blue."

"Nick. Look at me." I look her straight in the eyes, and she says, "The way I feel about you is the same."

"I know."

"So, what's changed?"

I can't tell her, and I can't even feel bad about it because it's not my fault I can't tell her, because I truly can't explain it. Something has shifted; something feels different.

"Nick. The way I feel about you is the same," she repeats.

And I say, looking at the carpet between my legs, "I don't think the way I feel about you is the same." The words taste terrible in my mouth, like something I should spit out.

I wait before looking back up at her. I wait as long as I can manage. Because when I look back up at her, her eyes are wet. They are shining so brightly that I think they have never looked more beautiful.

"You told me you loved me."

I don't say anything. I'm concentrating, trying to conjure up the feeling from the day after Thanksgiving. But I don't feel it. I can't remember what it feels like, and I'm surprised that something that felt so strong could disappear so quickly.

"Why would you say that?" Eden prompts.

"I don't know," I say finally.

"Bullshit," she says. "You can do better than that."

"I just can't feel it anymore," I say, and it's the truth.

"That doesn't mean it's not there anymore."

I shrug.

"What do you feel?"

I honestly don't know. But I don't feel good; and before, when I was with Eden, I felt so good, all the time.

"Nick, I think you're just completely overwhelmed by the way you feel about your dad right now," she says, and I can tell she's struggling to keep her voice even. "And I think that that's just making it impossible for you to feel anything else."

She leans in so that her head is so close to mine I can taste her breath when she talks. "I know you probably want to make your life go back to the way it was before you found out about Sam Roth, but you can't go back. And getting rid of me isn't going to make it any more like it was then."

"I'm not an idiot, Eden. I'm not trying to reverse the space-time continuum here. I know the difference between feeling something about my dad and feeling something about you."

She shakes her head. "No, I don't think you do."

I don't want to look at her anymore, but I don't want to look away, either.

"Nick," she says, "you've got to trust me, trust me about this."

"Trust you about what?"

"Nick—this—us—what we have—this is the lucky kind." Everything about her seems crinkled to me: her eyes, where she's trying to hold her tears so that she doesn't cry; her mouth, which she's set tightly; her voice, which is cracking. Even her hands, which she opens and shuts, in and out of fists, on her lap.

"The lucky kind?" I repeat.

"Remember when we said that there was the lucky kind and the unlucky kind?" I nod. I feel insanely like I'm a little kid who's behaved badly.

"Well, this, Nick, this is the lucky kind. You just have to trust me, and hang on to me." She takes my hands in between hers, and presses them together, and it feels like she's literally trying to hold us, our relationship, together, with both hands. She says, "I'll wait for you to catch on to what I already know."

I shake my head. "This has nothing to do with my dad."

"It does. You're just displacing your anxiety."

I look at her meanly. "What, did you read a psych textbook this afternoon?"

"I'm right, Nick. I'm right and you have to trust me." She's dropped my hands, and her fists are clenched in her lap now.

"You're wrong," I say, and I believe it. And so I get up to go. But I can still feel her touch on my hands; even hours later, my fingers are still warm where she'd pressed them together.

Step 9: Confirmation

You're not entirely sure what's just happened. As you walk to the subway, you think, Shit, did I just break up with Eden Reiss? But it's not until your best friend corners you after school the next day that you're sure.

"What's going on with Eden, man?" I'm crouched by my locker, looking for a textbook. I stand up, close the locker, and lean against it.

"What do you mean?" I say.

"She's white as a ghost today."

"It's the middle of winter. We're all white as ghosts."

"Dude, seriously."

"We had a fight yesterday."

"A fight?"

"I don't know if it was a fight. I don't know. But I told her that I didn't think that I felt the same way about her anymore."

"Why did you say that?" Stevie stands close to me, talking quietly.

"Because I don't."

"Since when?"

"Since I feel different, Stevie. Shit, what do you want me to say?" I want to bang my head against my locker, but I don't.

"You broke up with Eden Reiss," he says. He's not asking me; he's telling me.

"Yeah, I guess I did."

"Why?"

"I don't know, Stevie. Honestly, I don't," I say before he can jump down my throat. Stevie opens his mouth, and then shuts it. I can tell he has a dozen things he wants to say, questions he wants answered. I can't imagine talking anymore.

So I say, "Can we just—can we just stand here, quietly, until the bell rings, and then walk, quietly, home?"

"Yeah, we can do that," he says, and I'm surprised at how sympathetic he sounds, and he leans against the locker next to me, and presses my shoulder with his hand.

"Thank you," I say, and I really am grateful.

～

Congratulations, Reader. You've completed each of our tried-and-true steps, and have successfully ended your first—who knows, maybe your last—relationship.

We hope you're proud of yourself.

Studying

This week is finals week and next week we fly to Ohio, and I can't remember which week it is that I'm supposed to be preparing for.

European history. I know Eden will do better than I will. Chemistry. I know Stevie will do better than I will. And American literature. I'll do the best in that one. Since all that is predetermined, what difference does my studying or not make?

The thing is that I don't think I know how to study anymore. I know what I used to do: I used to sit on the sofa in the living room or on the floor in my room, and read over all my notes, look over the passages I'd highlighted in textbooks and novels. I'd sit there and I'd read for two hours at a time, sometimes more. But now, for the last week, I can't do it. I mean, I can still read. I can still carry my books around the house and lay them out just so.

But I can't sit still. I read one sentence: Henry the Eighth appealed to the pope for an annulment of his marriage to Catherine of Aragon. And then I try to keep reading. I look at the next sentence; I even know, more or less, what it will say: how the pope denied it, why the pope denied it, how many times Henry asked. But I can't read the next sentence. I have to stop. I have to stop because I am thinking about Eden, and all those nonfiction books she loved to read, and how she knew all about Henry the Eighth and Anne Boleyn before we ever took this class.

Or chemistry: I look over an experiment we did in class to show that when x and y combine, z occurs. I remember the experiment. I remember Stevie getting bored because we finished early, so he recited the whole periodic table with his eyes closed, and I made fun of him for being such a brainiac loser. But I can't read the conclusion of the experiment because I'm thinking about what happened when my dad and Sarah Booker combined, about the science that goes into making a baby. About X and Y chromosomes.

And then I'm thinking about Henry the Eighth again and how he was just trying to have a son and how much that has to do with X and Y chromosomes, and that makes me think of Sam Roth again, and then I can't even remember which subject I was supposed to have been studying.

But you'd never know I wasn't studying, because I'm sitting

there, with my books in my lap or on the coffee table in front of me, and I'm looking at them intently, carefully. I'm staring at them so hard I can't look away, concentrating so hard that when it's dinnertime, my mom has to call my name over and over again before I hear her. My parents don't even think much of the fact that Eden hasn't come over, and I haven't gone over there, because they just think we're studying so hard. They're probably proud of me for concentrating so hard on the task at hand.

I'm doing exactly what I'm supposed to be doing, but the only hope I have of doing well on these tests is that somehow the knowledge on the page will seep into my body through osmosis, since I'm definitely not reading it.

The night before finals the phone rings and I don't answer it, because even if I'm not studying, I'm trying to study, and I can't very well be trying to study if I'm also chatting on the phone. Picking up the phone is something you do when you are studying and you need a break. Which I certainly do not need and have not earned.

Although, I gotta say, even though I'm not studying, I'm exhausted. Trying to study and failing is much, much harder than actually studying.

"Nick!" I hear my mom yell from the other room.

"Yeah?"

"Phone!"

My dad would have come in; he would have told me who was calling. But my mom isn't as polite as he is. I pick up the phone. I assume that it'll be Stevie.

"Hello?"

"Hi." It's Eden. Her voice sounds shy somehow.

"Hi."

"How are you?"

"Fine." I don't ask how she is.

"How's studying going?"

Terribly. I can't stop thinking. But I say, "Fine."

"Good. That's good."

She doesn't say anything, so I finally say, "How about you—studying going well?"

"Terribly," she says, and her voice sounds like a piece of paper that's been balled up and left wrinkled. I'm selfishly relieved that she can't study, either, relieved that this is affecting her, too.

But she says, "My parents wanted to go out to dinner tonight. And I was, like, I can't, I'm studying, finals are tomorrow. And they said, Well, we have to talk to you, and I said, Well, can you do it inside the apartment, and they said, Okay. And then they sat me down and told me they had decided to get a divorce."

Well, that's not what I expected to hear, even though it's not a surprise.

"And now I can't tell if I'm upset because they're breaking up, or really angry at them because they told me the night before finals. I think it's 'cause they told me the night before finals. I mean, seriously, the news couldn't have waited another day? And it's not even like they could have forgotten, since I reminded them, right before they told me."

She's waiting for me to say something. "Wow, Eden," I say, sounding idiotic even to myself.

"I know," she says, and she's quiet for a minute, and I can hear her taking two long breaths. "And I just needed to tell someone."

"Well, you can tell me," I say, because it sounds like what a person should say at a time like this.

"I know," she says, and then she inhales like she's about to say something else, but she doesn't say anything but I don't hear her exhale, either, so we're just silent like that: I'm waiting until I can get off the phone, and she's holding whatever it is she wants to say in her mouth.

Finally, I say, "Well, I guess we should be studying, huh?"

"Yeah," she says, and she sounds disappointed. "I guess we should."

"Well, see you tomorrow," I say, like it's casual, like seeing her tomorrow is perfectly normal, even though it's not and it hasn't been for a few weeks now.

"Yeah," she says, "Good luck."

And then I put my books away. I close my notebooks and ready my school bag with pencils and erasers and pens. Preparing my bag is the most productive thing I'll do tonight.

Presents

Francis, in its infinite wisdom, schedules exams for the last day before break, so you cram them all into one day, and you don't have any idea how you did until school starts again in mid-January.

When I packed my bag last night, there was one thing I couldn't decide whether or not I needed, so I left it on the floor, next to my bag, just sitting there, like I thought that maybe I would put it in my bag this morning without thinking, or maybe I would forget it altogether.

It's Eden's Christmas present, so fat fucking chance.

I wrapped it weeks ago. Before Thanksgiving, even. I

wrapped it and I hid it in my closet where she wouldn't find it. It's a scarf. It really is. It's a beautiful new lady's scarf, and folded up inside it is my scarf, the one she always liked to steal, the one I'm sure she's noticed I haven't been wearing lately, because it's in my closet, folded up neatly and waiting for her.

I was actually thrilled when I thought to give it to her, relieved to have come up with the perfect present. Now I don't think I can give it to her, but I also can't ever wear it again, because it's already hers. I'd be wearing Eden's scarf if I wore it.

So I don't wear it, even though my neck is friggin' freezing lately.

I'm holding the present when I walk into the living room in the morning, trying to decide, still, whether to put it in my backpack. My dad's sitting at his desk, staring at the computer screen. I don't even notice him until he says, "What you got there?"

"Huh?" I say, blinking. My dad's still pretty careful with me these days. He hesitates before he asks me a question; he sounds nervous when he does. We're getting along, but I think we both know that the slightest misstep could ruin it, and seeing as we're leaving for Ohio tomorrow night, I think my dad is particularly scared.

"In your hand," he says. "The present." It's so obviously a present. The wrapping paper has Christmas trees on it and everything.

"Oh, this?" I say, lifting it slightly. "It's Eden's Christmas present."

"Oh. First present," my dad says knowingly. "Big step."

"Yeah," I say, and now I stuff it in my bag, wrinkling up the paper. "Better go, I guess."

"Good luck today, Buddy."

"Thanks," I say, as though there's any chance I'm not going to do terribly today. I sling my bag over my shoulder and it feels like it weighs eighty pounds.

Stevie is waiting for me in the lobby. We walk to school without talking. I've gotten Eden the heaviest scarf in the world, I think as I limp along with my back hunched. But I don't have to give it to her. Just 'cause it's in my bag. I can stuff it inside my locker, no problem.

But then when we get to school, Eden's waiting at my locker. So there's no way I can get it in there without her seeing it. I'll keep it in my bag.

"Hey," I say.

"Hey," she answers.

Stevie asks her how she's doing, and they chat about the tests, and maybe Eden tells him about her parents, I can't be sure. I'm just looking at her, leaning on my locker. Finally, I say, to get her to move more than anything else, "I need to get in there."

And then, because I am, after all, an enormous idiot, I open my fucking bag to put some of my books inside my locker. And so, of course Eden sees the wrapping paper, and Stevie sees it, and even if I don't give it to her, everyone knows about it now.

"I wrapped it before," I say, and that's as much as I explain. I hand her the present and shut my locker, and Stevie and I walk away, to take our tests. I know Stevie wants to stay with her, make sure she's okay, stand next to her while she decides whether or not to open the present, squeeze her arm if it makes her cry, but instead he comes with me, even though we both know that I'm an asshole.

'Twas the Night Before the Night Before Christmas

Usually, we fly to Ohio on Christmas Day. Usually, Stevie comes over on Christmas Eve and we have a big dinner, and then he helps us load all our stuff into a cab in the morning. This year, we're flying a day early. My dad says it was more to do with the flights than Sam Roth, but I'm guessing Sam Roth has at least something to do with it.

Stevie comes home with me after finals; he's staying over just like he would if it were Christmas Eve.

"Don't you think we're getting a little old for sleepovers?" I ask as I make up a bed for him on my floor.

"You say that every year," Stevie says.

"I know. Doesn't seem to get truer the more I say it, though."

Stevie shakes his head and grins. "Nope."

When we were little, we'd try to stay up until midnight, even though we didn't believe in Santa, even though my apartment doesn't even have chimneys, even though we had to get up early on Christmas Day. It used to be hard to make ourselves stay up so late. Now it's after midnight and I can't sleep.

Stevie's voice surprises me in the darkness; I thought he'd been sleeping.

"Dude, just 'cause you can't sleep, could you tone down the tossing and turning for the rest of us?"

"The rest of us?" I repeat irritably.

"Those of us who didn't just dump our dream girl. Those of us who aren't being kept awake by thoughts of how much more comfortable the bed would be if only she were in it."

I can't think of a comeback. After a few seconds of silence, Stevie laughs, "Can't even deny it, can you, champ?"

"Just shut up for a few minutes."

"You're the one making all that noise."

"I know," I say. "I'll try to hold still." And it's pathetic, but the only way that I can get comfortable is by holding my pillow in front of me, like I'm spooning it; like I'm spooning Eden. How can I be uncomfortable without her in my bed when we never even spent the night together? How can I smell her shampoo on my pillows when the sheets have been changed since she was last here? How can I miss her, when I'm the one who broke up with her?

I bet she opened the present I gave her. I bet she wondered whether it would be more distracting to wait until after finals to open it or to open it first: should she obsess over what she knew it was or over what she thought it might be? I think she opened it first. I hope she only saw the scarf on the outside; then she could even be a little disappointed that I hadn't been able to come up with anything better, anything more personal. I hope she waited until after finals to unfold it and see the other scarf wrapped up inside.

I should have just left the present in my closet. Only an asshole would give her an emotionally charged present five minutes before finals, the morning after her parents told her they were splitting. And I never used to be such an asshole.

But I also wonder whether I left some scent on my scarf, the way she's left hers on my pillows. I think of all the months I spent imagining what her different smells and tastes would be like; now I've spent so much time with them that they've made their way under my covers, into the mattress, and deep into the down filling of my pillows.

And I wonder whether she's smelling me on my scarf, and thinking of me, just like I'm thinking of her. But then, only a bigger asshole hopes that the girl he broke up with has yet to get over him.

～

In the morning, we leave for the airport at six. Stevie always gets up with us so that he and Pilot can say good-bye. My parents give us presents, then Stevie watches me pack.

"Don't you think you should have done this last night?"

"Don't you think you'd be more useful if you weren't sitting on top of the pile of clothes I need to put into the suitcase?"

"Don't snap at me just 'cause you're so nervous about meeting your new big bro that you broke up with the girl you loved."

I glare at him. "Don't psychoanalyze me, Stevie. You don't understand."

He shrugs. "Yeah, well, neither do you."

Stevie doesn't usually give in so easily. I realize that we're sending him back to his apartment with our dog to spend Christmas Eve alone. I don't even know if his parents are in town.

"Dude, are your parents going to be around tonight?"

He shrugs. "I doubt it."

"It's Christmas Eve."

"They're Jewish; they don't care."

"So are we."

"It's not the same. Not every family is a Norman Rockwell painting on Christmas Eve."

"Well, mine's not, not anymore."

Stevie shakes his head at me. "Dude, it really still is. You just got an extra person painted in there this year."

"It's more complicated than that."

"I know," Stevie says seriously. "And look, I respect your right to be pissed at your parents for springing your new big bro on you after sixteen years of staying mum on the subject. But one of these days you're going to have to snap out of it. Look at what Eden's parents did to her the other night. Look at . . ."

He lets his voice trail off, and the room is quiet while I wonder whether Stevie was about to say, Look at my parents, who didn't even notice that this year I'm all alone on Christmas Eve.

Finally, I say, "I don't think big bro is quite the right name for it."

Stevie shrugs. "Guess the English language is failing you on this one, pal."

I zip up my case. "There's not a word in the world for what he is. He's someone else's son, but my dad is his father. He's not my brother, but we have the same parent. But stepbrother and half brother sound wrong, too."

"You'd think the adoption people would have come up with something by now."

"Something more succinct than biological family."

"Something pithier, like bio-bro."

"Sounds like a superhero," I say. "Bio-Bro swooping in to save the day."

"At least you've finally got a sense of humor about it," Stevie says, clapping me on the back.

Stevie loves to act like he's older than I am, wiser.

"Dude, I'm about to get one new big-brother-type in my life. I don't need another."

Flying

I love airports. Especially at Christmas when it's crowded and everyone's hurrying, carrying extra bags full of presents that will inevitably be crushed before they reach their destinations. I love it because they're all going somewhere: back home, or on vacation to someplace tropical, excited to go someplace new, or to meet someone new.

This trip has never been new. By the time I was old enough to understand what an airport was and where we were going, I'd already been on this trip so many times that it was familiar. So it is very strange to be anxious now, at the airport, watching my mom pick out magazines and buy gum while my dad loads up on snacks. He always buys junk food before a flight, as though he thinks there's a chance the flight might last for days and days and he needs to make sure we won't starve up there.

He should be more nervous, certainly. At least, he should be more nervous than I am. But he doesn't seem anxious at all: He's humming while he grabs Reese's Peanut Butter Cups; he keeps taking my mom's hand and kissing it; he even tousled my hair as we got into the cab.

No, he's not nervous. He's like a kid going to Disney World for the first time: He knows what's there, he's seen the commercials, he's looked through the brochures and planned out which rides he's going to go on and which characters he's going to meet. But all that preparation hasn't prepared him for the actual thrill of going on Space Mountain, and now it's all he can think about.

I wonder if he was that excited when my mom was pregnant with me. I wonder if he held her hand in the cab on the way to the hospital, got candy at the gift shop, tapped his feet on the floor in the delivery room.

～♡

We do the same things at the airport every year. The candy and magazines are first, and I'm ready now to move on to the next thing: coffee from the greasy-looking Starbucks next to the security line.

"Hey, Dad," I say, "think you can tear yourself away from the candy long enough to grab a latte?"

He looks surprised at the suggestion. We've been doing this forever; when I was too young for coffee, it was hot chocolate.

"Sure, Buddy," he says. He hands his candy to Mom, and we walk to Starbucks.

On line, he sways back and forth next to me, like he's dancing to a song only he can hear. His head bops from one side to the other. He looks like those men in old movies, the ones in the hospital waiting room, waiting for their children to be born.

"Do you want caramel on yours?" I ask, and he nods, looking off ahead of me. I even have to pay, since he's so distracted he just walks away when the barista rings up our order.

He walks ahead of me to the gate, and I follow him with our drinks. I feel like a waiter.

"Thanks, Buddy," he says when I hand him his drink. He takes a sip and looks out the window; I don't know if it's holding the warm drink or looking at the orderly way the planes outside are arranged, but he seems calmer now.

He says, "Look at all those planes lining up. It seems more crowded every year; more people coming home."

Especially this year, I think as I take a sip of my drink. My father is still looking out the window as he says, "I think, Buddy, I think I may owe you an apology."

I don't say anything. I look at the planes, too.

"I don't know, honestly, what I should have done differently, when I might have told you sooner, or how I should have told you."

I nod. I don't know what the right way would have been, either.

"When I signed up for the registry, you were so young. And then the years passed, and he never called. I ignored your mother—she thought I should have told you years ago. But I had started to think he was never going to call. I couldn't see the point in telling you when he hadn't called.

"I never should have put you in a position where you were going to answer the phone one night and have it be the baby I gave up. I can't see any way around it, but I should have found a way."

I nod. I notice that he still refers to the nearly thirty-year-old man whose name we now know as the baby he gave up. Maybe Sam will be a baby until tomorrow, when my father sees that he is a grown person.

I say, "I didn't know it was him at the time."

"Yeah, but afterward. You might have had flashbacks," he says, and he smiles. It's a lame joke, and not very funny, but I'm grateful to my dad for making it, since it makes the lump in my throat recede.

"Anyway, Buddy," my dad says, "I just wanted to tell you that. I don't want you to think you weren't foremost in my mind when I decided that I wanted to meet Sam, or when Sam and I started talking. I was already thinking about you the very day we gave Sam up, before you and I had even met. I was already worried about how it might impact the family I'd have someday. I wish I could have thought of a better way to have done all this."

I nod. I wish I'd done it better, too, I say to him silently.

Dad reaches into his pocket to make sure the tickets are there. Then panic crosses his face when they're not, followed by relief when he remembers he gave them to my mom to hold, followed by panic when he realizes that if Mom is holding them, he can't check to make sure they're still there. And then I laugh, out loud. Even if I'm not a part of it, I can't remember the last time I saw my father so excited.

On the plane, I pretend to sleep. When I close my eyes, I see Eden's face, and she's smiling at me. Much to my surprise, seeing her makes me feel better, makes me calm. And I wish, I really do wish, that she were here, sitting next to me on the plane, holding my hand throughout this strange and radically new trip we're taking.

Ohio

Sam won't actually be here until sometime tomorrow. He's spending Christmas Eve with his real family, I guess. His other family. Or maybe his fiancée's family.

"Is his fiancée coming?" I ask.

"No, he wanted to come by himself."

"Where is he staying?" I ask. We're decorating the tree in my grandparents' living room.

"The same Days Inn where we're staying," Dad answers quickly, because it's obvious. It's the only hotel close by.

"How come we never stay with Grandma and Grandpa?"

I never thought to ask that before. We've always stayed in the same place.

"We never have, not since I married your mother."

"Why?"

"It just seemed easier for everyone involved." He reaches down for a bell-shaped ornament. "My mother was already putting so much into getting the house ready for Christmas, it didn't seem fair to ask her to play hostess any more than that."

I have other questions. I ask two at once, rapid-fire. "How did Grandma and Grandpa react when you told them about Sam Roth? When did you tell them?"

"Well, your grandmother already knew—I told her when he was born—I didn't tell your grandfather until I knew Sam was coming for Christmas. But he told me he'd suspected it."

"He did?"

"Yeah—could have knocked me over with a feather. But I guess there are some things sons can't hide from fathers without their at least suspecting it."

He doesn't look at me when he says it; he's looking at the ornaments in his hand, like he has to decide whether to put Charlie Brown or the rocking horse on the tree first. But I look at him, and I watch him hang them both, and I wonder whether he's really talking about his dad, or whether he's trying to tell me he knows about Eden and me; knows that I loved her, and knows that I left her.

"When did you tell them he was coming for Christmas?" I ask.

"Around Thanksgiving."

"Before or after you told me?" I ask, feeling my face get hot; it's really quite something how quickly it turns out I can get angry. I must find a way to put this skill to good use. Wrestling. Acting. Politics.

"After. Jesus, Nick, you know that—I told you that."

"You did?" I try to remember; he came into my room, he was going to ask me my opinion.

"When you called me snotty," I say slowly.

"Well, you were being snotty at the time," he says, but then he smiles at me.

"Right."

"You used to think before you spoke, I think."

"I used to," I agree, and we leave it at that.

The Days Inn

When I was little, my parents and I shared a room at the Days Inn. I've never been so relieved to be a teenager as I am tonight, when I get to go into a room with a different key, all my own, and pick up my phone to call Stevie.

"Hey," I say, lying against the pillows and propping my feet up.

"Hey, Christmas Boy, how are things in the Midwest?"

"Is this considered the Midwest?"

"Sure it is."

"Oh."

"Do you even know what the capital of Ohio is?"

"Should I?"

"Dude, we learned the state capitals in fifth grade."

"Well, we learned long division in the fifth grade and that sure has come in handy since they began letting us use a calculator."

"Sure has."

I lean my head back against the wall behind me. "What's going on back in NYC?"

"It's cold as balls, I'll tell you that."

"Wait, does that actually mean it's hot? Like when people say cold as hell; shouldn't that actually mean it's hot?"

"You are much too easily confused these days, my friend. It's just an expression."

"Whatever. What'd you do today?"

"Well, I'll tell you."

"Please do."

Stevie actually hesitates before saying, "I went to the movies with Eden."

I look up at the ceiling. The paint is peeling. I imagine that if I sleep with my mouth open tonight, pieces will fall in and I'll get lead poisoning.

"Nicholas?" Stevie prompts.

"Yeah, okay. What movie?"

"Does that matter?"

"I guess not."

"Aren't you going to at least ask the obvious questions?"

"They must not be so obvious 'cause I don't know which questions those are."

"Let's start out with: How is she doing?"

"Okay," I comply, "how is she doing?"

"Bad, man. Really bad."

"I'm so glad I asked."

"I'm not telling you to make you feel bad."

"Then why?"

" 'Cause I thought you might like to know, seeing as until a few mysterious weeks ago she was the love of your life."

"Okay. Tell me."

"Her parents are being real assholes. They keep taking her aside and telling her the terrible things the other did. Lying, cheating, money—you name it."

"Wow."

"And you know how chill she can be, but she's just, like, these are things she'd have been better off not knowing, you know?"

"I know."

"And she doesn't have anyone to tell about it."

"She's telling you."

"Only 'cause you left her high and dry."

"Don't say that. She's got plenty of friends."

"She wants to talk to you."

"Well, she could call me."

I can practically hear Stevie shaking his head. "No, I don't think she could. When she called to tell you that her parents were splitting, you weren't exactly warm and fuzzy."

"Dude, it was the night before finals. I was studying. And anyway, how do you know that?"

"How the fuck do you think I know it? She needs to talk to someone; she's worried about you."

"I'm fine."

"Oh yeah, you're stellar," Stevie laughs. "Dude, you should never sleep with a girl so soon after learning that your dad got some girl pregnant. And certainly not on the very day you learned that you're going to come face to face with said progeny."

I run my hands through my hair, swinging my legs over the side of the bed so that my feet are firmly planted on the floor.

"Jesus Christ, is there anything that girl hasn't told you?"

"Don't be mad at her."

I shake my head. "I'm not."

"You made some stupid-assed decisions in the last few weeks."

I press my feet into the cheap carpet, hard.

"I don't know," I say.

"Well, I do. See what happens when you fly blind? You've gotta run the major plays by me first."

I smile. I'm thankful Stevie has made a joke. "Yeah, I'm sure that would have helped enormously."

"No doubt."

"I'm glad you're looking out for her," I say.

"Dude, I'm only a seat filler. She needs you."

I press my eyes closed so tight that my head starts to ache. "Yeah, well, let's just—we'll see."

"That we will, my friend. That we will."

Christmas Day

When I wake up, the first thing I think of is my father at the airport: foot-tapping, hair-tousling, smiling.

I am none of those things. I am what I would have thought my father would be: a nervous wreck. In the shower, I can't hold on to anything—the soap slips out of my hand; the shampoo clatters against the wall so loudly I actually listen for the sound of the proprietors banging on the door to see if I've broken their hotel. And then I actually fall when I get out of the shower. I grab on to the curtain for support and it rips, but just a little, enough that maybe no one will notice, and then I wonder if that's like a double sin, to break something on Christmas Day and hope no one notices.

And that's when I remember it's Christmas. That's when I remember that today is not just Sam's day. My grandparents will have stacked presents under the tree, my father will drink eggnog by the gallon, my mother will have written cards to each of us, my grandmother will have made a turkey and stuffing, and the house will smell like cinnamon.

Christ, I think, Sam will think he's walking into a fucking Norman Rockwell painting.

I imagine, actually, that that would make him angry: *These are the people who gave me up*, he'll think. *These* people? They could have kept me. They're not poor, they're not drug-addled, they're not incapable. What, he'll think, they just couldn't be *bothered*?

That's what I think I would think.

We rented two cars: one so that my mom and I can head over to Grandma's, and one for my dad to take to the airport. So that he can pick up Sam, alone. I'm surprised to discover that I wish I were in the car with him. Just out of curiosity. I don't want to participate, but I do want to see.

Then again, maybe not. Maybe they'll hug and cry, and maybe he'll look exactly like my dad and I won't be able to tell which one is which, and maybe then I'll stick out like a sore thumb. Surely, at least, Sam, being from Texas, will fit in better here than I do, being from New York City.

But there I am, being snotty again.

In the car on the way to my grandparents', I fiddle with the radio. There are surprisingly good radio stations in Ohio. I find one playing music my mom likes and turn up the volume. She looks over at me and smiles. "Thanks for that, Nicky."

I shrug. "Well, you know, gotta be nice to you on Christmas."

"Next year maybe you'll tackle the drive from the Days Inn."

I look at her, surprised. She started complaining about my taking driver's ed the second I turned sixteen. I've always thought that she's the one who babies me most: She can't fall asleep until I get home; she tells me what to wear and metes out punishment when I drink; she can't stand the thought of me behind the wheel; she literally refers to me as her baby. But then, she was the one who didn't want to keep me in the dark.

"Mom," I say slowly, "thank you, by the way."

"What for?"

"Dad told me that you thought I should have already known about Sam—you said he should have told me years ago."

She doesn't say anything for a minute; she looks intently at the road. She hates to tell me when she and Dad disagree; her parents fought all the time when she was growing up.

Finally, she says, "I didn't like having a secret. It made sense when you were younger, but then . . ." She stops talking as we turn in to my grandparents' driveway. She unbuckles her seat belt and turns to face me. "You're doing a pretty good job growing up, Nicky. You know that, right?"

I blush and look at the house in front of us. "Mom, just 'cause it's Christmas and I let you listen to Carly Simon, let's not get all touchy-feely."

She grins at me. "You're right," she says, "let's not. This day's going to be emotional enough as it is." She closes her eyes for a second, and it suddenly occurs to me that maybe she's just as intimidated by this day as I am. She leans over and quickly kisses my cheek and then steps out of the car before I have the chance to say anything else.

My grandparents seem pretty nervous. My grandmother always cooks too much, but I convince myself that this year she made even more. My mother puts her hand on my shoulder, and I can feel through my T-shirt that her palm is sweaty. I go into my grandfather's study and check my email. Then I look up the news to see what's going on in the rest of the world. Anything to remind me that the whole world is bigger than my own world, and that much more exciting and important things are going on out there than in here. But then, like everyone else in the house, I hear a car crunching onto the gravel driveway. I force myself to stay put, stay sitting at the computer. I will not run out to the living room, near the front door, where everyone else is waiting. I will stay right here.

I hear the front door open, and then I hear that my father is making introductions. I hear a deep voice, much deeper than my dad's, say "Merry Christmas, Mr. Brandt" to my grandfather and then "You have a lovely home, Mrs. Brandt" to my grandmother. And I hear my mother laughing, and I hear him call her Nina, and there is such familiarity in his voice that I know he and my mother have talked before.

"Where's Nick?" my dad says. I imagine he's pulling off his coat and taking Sam's, and leaving them on the chair in the doorway. I know my grandmother will hang them up later, when no one is looking.

"Nick!" my dad shouts, and I can't delay any longer. I think that since this will be the last time I stand up without knowing what my father's firstborn looks like, I should do it slowly. I push my grandfather's chair out from under his desk, feeling the wood scratch the carpet underneath it. My stomach hurts, and I will be very pissed if Sam's being here spoils my appetite because I love Christmas food. And that's the thought in my head when I walk into the living room.

I see my father first—he's standing in front of Sam—and he's smiling, and looking at me excitedly. Maybe he's been waiting for this moment as much as he was waiting to meet Sam.

And then he steps aside, but before I see Sam's face I see his hands. And then his hands are all I see because I recognize them; he has my father's hands, which means he has my hands, which apparently means that I can't tear my gaze away from his hands, can't be bothered to look at his face, even with all this curiosity. I think I would have known him anywhere, just by his hands.

"Nick, this is Sam," my dad says as I walk toward them. I wonder if Sam will hug me. I don't know whether he hugged my grandparents—his grandparents—hello, or my mom (his stepmom?). I don't know if he hugged my dad. My dad is pretty big on hugging. He puts his arm around me now as he introduces me.

"Nice to meet you, Nick," Sam says, and he doesn't go to hug me but instead to shake my hand, and luckily, since I'm staring at his hands, I see that, and I reach out my hand to shake his. And it's when our fingers meet that I am finally able to look up, and at his face.

He doesn't look like my dad. He's taller, like I am, and much tanner, I guess from all the Texas sun. His hair is lighter than ours, and his teeth look very white and very straight. But he does have my father's eyes, maybe not quite the same color, but the shape of them, the way they crinkle at the sides as he smiles when he shakes my hand. But I honestly don't think I would have noticed that unless I'd been looking.

I don't know what I thought he would look like, but I'm relieved to see that this is it.

"Nice to meet you," I say back, the same reflex that reminded me to reach for his hand when he offered it.

"You too," he says, even though he's already said it.

My grandmother ushers us inside. We haven't opened any presents yet. I kind of feel like we shouldn't, not with a guest here, but my grandmother insists. Sam sits next to my dad on the couch. I look at them more than I look at my presents, even though I feel bad because I know how my grandmother agonizes over what to get me every year.

I feel a little ridiculous saying this, but Sam is really effing handsome. It's like having a blond Superman sitting on your grandparents' couch. Bio-Bro indeed, I think wryly. My dad can't take his eyes off him. I think how proud he must be, having made something that came out so well. But then, I think, my dad would probably be looking at him like that no matter what Sam looked like. I've caught my father looking at me like that, too. But there's something else in my father's face; I think he's relieved. Relieved to see that the baby he gave away is all grown-up, and seems to have grown up well, and happily. Relieved that his bad luck doesn't seem to have turned into Sam's bad luck. It makes me understand a little better why my dad was so excited to meet him, so excited every time he called.

My grandmother keeps going back to the tree to grab and distribute presents. She walks over to hand one to my dad and, much to my surprise, places one in Sam's lap. "From Santa," she says, the same way she still says it to me. Sam looks so surprised that I almost think he's going to cry. He looks to my dad, for permission, I guess, to unwrap it. My father nods, smiling, and Sam undoes the string around the box. It's a scarf from Banana Republic. I recognize it; I tried it on when I was looking for a scarf to replace the one I gave to Eden. A pretty impersonal gift, I guess, but from the look on Sam's face, you'd think it was the greatest thing anyone ever gave him.

After dinner, just like on Thanksgiving, we play board games—today it's Trivial Pursuit. For the first time, I think how lame our traditions must be to an outsider. Funny, I didn't think that when Eden came at Thanksgiving, and I've never thought that about Stevie, but then it feels like Stevie has always been there, and it felt like Eden was always supposed to have been there.

Dad says he and Sam will be a team before anyone can say anything else. I guess he wanted to make sure Sam wouldn't feel left out. Usually I play with Dad and my mom plays with one or both of my grandparents, but tonight they're staying in the kitchen, taking their time cleaning up.

We sit around the coffee table in the living room. It doesn't take long before my mom and I are creaming Sam and Dad. The funny thing is, though, they're losing on things that I know my dad knows—he just can't remember. We've been playing this same version of Trivial Pursuit for years (my grandparents refuse to buy a new one, and even though we always say we'll bring an updated version from home, we never do). So half the time, Dad and Sam are getting questions that we had last year or the year before—questions that maybe you don't remember right away, but then when you talk it out, you remember. That's how my mom and I are winning. That's how Dad and I won last year.

Sam can't, obviously, play like that. He doesn't laugh, like the rest of us do, when my dad gets a question about cereal and answers Grape-Nuts, just because that's his favorite. Sam doesn't know how often it happens that my dad's random guesses are true, that you want him on your team because he has good luck, or that you want my mom on your team because she always knows the most arcane of facts.

Less than an hour goes by and my mom and I have three pie pieces, and they only have one. My grandparents want us to come back to the table for dessert, and my dad claps Sam on his back when they stand up from the sofa, as if to say Nice try and Good game. But he leans in toward me as we walk to the dining room and whispers, "That's the last time I let myself get separated from you, old man." And I almost laugh: Sam is really no competition.

~○

I ride with my mother back to the Days Inn. Sam and Dad are still in their separate car. I wonder what they're talking about. Has Sam asked him why, with such a supportive and understanding family, he gave him up to begin with?

At the hotel, they've lost Sam's reservation, and believe it or not the Days Inn of Troy, Ohio, is booked solid.

"Lots of people come to visit their families," Dad guesses.

We're standing in the lobby. I want badly to get to my room, turn off the lights, and watch some bad Christmas movies. I want to be alone. My dad has actually raised his voice to the woman behind the check-in desk, for which he immediately apologized. I can tell he feels guilty, as though he can't actually believe that he yelled at someone who has to work on Christmas Day. Sam is hanging on to his duffel bag for dear life. I know what I'm supposed to say, but the words are sandpapery in my mouth as I say them:

"Sam can stay in my room."

My dad looks at me. "Are you sure, Buddy?" he asks.

"Sure," I say, though really I'm thinking, Well, what's the alternative? "Come on," I say to Sam. The Days Inn is one of those motels where you climb rickety outdoor metal stairs to get to your room. I lead the way up the stairs and fit the key in the lock. I can tell Sam wants some privacy, to take out his phone and call his fiancée, to digest everything that's happened today. I should offer to go wait outside, but it's freezing.

Sam sits on the couch in my room.

"They said it opens up," I offer. "And there's extra bedding in the closet."

"Okay," Sam says, and I sit and watch him make the bed. There is something eerily brotherly about it.

"Do you smoke?" Sam asks.

I shrug. "At parties."

"That's how I started," he says. "I've almost quit, but I bought a pack on my way here. Haven't opened it yet. Didn't want Rob to smell it on me and think I was a smoker."

I think it's funny he said "Rob" instead of "your dad."

"Yeah, he hates smoking," I say.

"Yeah," he agrees, and I'm thinking how much my dad would hate it if he knew either of us, let alone both of us, was currently aching for a cigarette. I'm waiting for Sam to say he's going to go out and smoke one—it'll get him out of the room, out of my eye line and earshot, and I'm sure he'd like that. But instead he says, "Wanna go outside?"

He digs the cigarettes out of his duffel bag and holds the pack out, an invitation.

I shrug. "Okay, sure."

Cigarettes with Sam

It's cold, but I'm guessing that Sam is one of those outdoorsy kinds of guys who aren't bothered by the cold. He hands me a cigarette, but every time he holds the lighter to it, the wind blows out the flame.

"Here, give it to me," he says, and then he puts my cigarette, and a second, in his mouth, and stands close to the brick wall of the Days Inn, his back to me. He turns around and both cigarettes are lit. He hands me one.

I take it, but I hesitate for a second before putting it in my mouth. Sam doesn't notice; he's closed his eyes and is taking a long drag. I remember that when I was little, I thought it was only okay to share forks and knives and drinks with someone you were related to. I thought with everyone else it was dirty, but with family you didn't have to worry about sharing germs.

Sam exhales and opens his eyes. If he notices that I haven't smoked the cigarette he's given me, he doesn't let on.

"Let's walk," he says, heading for the stairs. I follow him, carefully placing the cigarette between my lips.

Sam walks slowly, his long legs loping down the stairs and toward the parking lot. I want to make a list of the things I know about him now.

"Do you have any brothers or sisters?" I ask.

Sam answers without stopping, without looking back at me, "Nope. Only child."

"Is that why your parents adopted? They couldn't get pregnant?"

"Couldn't get pregnant. When I was little, before I could really understand what it meant to be adopted, I used to beg them to get me a little brother. I thought it'd be such fun to be someone's older brother."

That seems like a loaded statement, so I wait a beat before saying anything.

"I'm an only child, too," I finally offer.

"I know," he says. I wonder how much about my life my father has told him.

"You're a junior," he says as we walk across the parking lot. There's a bench at the far end, near the main entrance to the hotel. I assume that's where we're headed.

"Yeah."

"I was a junior when I met Cath."

"Who's Cath?" I ask dumbly.

"Catherine. My fiancée," he says, but not like he thought I should have known.

"You're marrying your high school sweetheart?"

He looks back at me and grins. "Pretty lame, huh?"

Even though it's cold, I feel my face getting hot: I'm blushing.

"Sometimes you meet the right one early, I guess," he says.

"I guess."

"How about you?" he asks. "You got a girl?"

I shake my head, looking away. My nose is running. When we reach the bench, Sam sits; I stay standing.

"Can I have another cigarette?" I ask finally. I'd tossed the other one halfway across the parking lot after I finished it.

"Sure," he says, and lights two more. He doesn't even offer me the chance to light it myself, like he assumes he can do it better.

"I was such a fuckup when we dated in high school," he says, shifting his weight on the bench. I still haven't sat down. "I'd always known that I was adopted, but I got so fucked up about it then."

"What do you mean?"

"You know, I didn't know who they were then. I had this picture in my mind that they must have been in high school. You know, the typical story." He looks away as he smokes. "High school kids who don't think they need to be careful, who get in trouble, who don't know what else to do, that kind of thing."

"Yeah," I say, and I sit down now, next to him.

"But Cath, she was so much smarter than I was. I tried to break up with her all the time."

"Really?" I try to sound nonchalant, but I'm riveted.

"Yeah. Especially after we had sex, can you believe it? I mean, whoever heard of a teenage boy doing that—avoiding more sex?"

"Crazy," I say, and my voice is hoarse.

"I thought whatever we felt for each other couldn't be the real thing; it was a total joke, because what did teenagers know about life if they made stupid mistakes like the people who had me must have made? I told her that our love wasn't real."

"What did she say?" I ask, and I actually lean toward him to make sure I don't miss any of the answer.

"She would just tell me that I was wrong. She said some people find the real thing when they're young. And if you do, you're lucky."

Sam takes another drag on his cigarette, a long one, but I don't say anything; I'm hoping Catherine said more. Sam continues, "And she'd say that maybe the people who had me were the lucky kind—maybe they really loved each other."

Sam pauses now, like he's remembering one of these exchanges with Catherine; and he half smiles, like he's thinking of the boy he was, the one who was so foolish that he tried to turn his back on love, and so lucky he found a girl who wouldn't let him.

"And we would break up and make up—we'd have the most ridiculous fights and I'd say terrible things. But the breakups just didn't take. I always came back. And every time we got back together, I'd believe it that I really was lucky." He smiles. "And not just because she took me back, you know?"

I know I'm supposed to say something, but I can't talk. I can't talk because a golf ball has found its way into my throat. I try to smoke, but even the smoke can't get past the golf ball. I start coughing and I can't stop. It feels like I'll never be able to take a deep breath again.

"Shit, Nick, are you okay?" Sam says, patting my back. "Shit, some brother I would have made, huh? I've already got you smoking and choking."

But I'm not choking. I'm crying. I'm crying so hard my eyes hurt and mucus is running down my chin. I haven't cried like this since I was a kid, and I can't stop crying. Oh shit, I'm crying in front of Sam Roth. I don't want him to think he's the reason why.

"It's not because of you," I choke out, finally.

"What?"

"I'm not so freaked out by meeting you that I'm crying."

"I didn't think you were."

I take a deep breath. "I just miss my girlfriend, that's all."

"You said you didn't have a girlfriend."

I shake my head, wiping my nose. "I did. Before."

"Before when?"

"Before I became such a fuckup," I say, echoing his words, trying to laugh.

"Well, shit, here I've been your big brother for, like, four hours and you're already copying me." Sam grins.

I am finally able to take a deep breath. I wipe my eyes.

"That's not the right name for what you are," I say, but I'm not angry that he said it.

"I know," he says. "I just don't know what the right thing to call it is."

"At least you made it into a joke."

Sam grins. "It just so happens that I am one of the funniest people you will ever meet."

I look at his smile. "You know your teeth are freakishly white, right?" I say.

Sam puts his fingers over his lips, trying to cover his smile.

"Cath. She wanted me to whiten them before the wedding. Smoker's teeth, you know. Yellow."

"I guess we know who'll be wearing the pants in the Roth household." I should be colder now; my face is soaking wet from crying. But I feel warm.

Sam laughs, leaning back. He claps me on the back. "All I can say is thank God for the women in our lives."

And I nod. I nod because the women in our lives really do know best.

The Sights and Sounds
of Troy, Ohio

I t's raining when we wake up the next morning, but Dad has promised Sam a tour of his old neighborhood—the school, the mall, his favorite restaurants. I wonder whether he'll show him where Sarah Booker lived.

This is the first night I've slept straight through since Eden and I broke up. When I wake up, Sam is in the bathroom with the door closed. I realize later that it was the sound of the shower, not the rain outside, that actually woke me. He emerges fully dressed, with wet hair.

"Did I wake you?" he says, but not apologetically.

"Uh-uh," I say.

Sam looks at me and says, "I'm going to get you some ice."

"What for?" I say. I want to go deeper under the covers but I force myself to sit up instead.

"Your eyes are red," he says, grabbing the cardboard bucket on the dresser and heading out the door. "I'll be right back."

In the bathroom, with the door closed behind me, I look in the mirror and see that Sam was understating it. My eyes aren't just red but puffed out, swollen, like I'm a little kid who woke up crying from a nightmare in the middle of the night. No nightmare here, I think, just my life.

Okay, so maybe I'm being a little bit melodramatic. I probably just look stoned. I turn on the water for the shower.

"I'm leaving the ice by the door," I hear Sam say. I open the bathroom door just enough to reach my arm out and grab the bucket. I bring the whole thing into the shower, making the water as hot as I can. Then I close my eyes and press an ice cube over each one until it's so cold it hurts. Sam would probably know a better way to do it.

When I get out of the shower, I can hear Sam and Dad talking in the outer room. Going over plans for the day. Discussing breakfast. I gather I have the option of either going back to my grandparents' with my mom or tagging along with them. I guess they'd probably prefer to have the day to themselves; maybe there are things they want to use the time to discuss. Sam leaves late tonight, so this is their only real time together.

I decide I want to go with them.

In the car, Dad apologizes for the weather, as though he ought to have been able to arrange for it to be better. I'm sitting in the backseat, and every so often Dad glances at me in the rearview mirror, like I'm a little kid in a car seat.

If Eden were here, she would think it was sweet, the way Dad looks back to check on me. If Eden were here, I would slide my hand across the seat and press the side of my hand against hers. Then I would lace her fingers through mine, and squeeze.

Maybe Sam told him about what happened last night, how I cried. Maybe he thinks my dad would be happy to hear how we bonded, or maybe he thought he had to tell my dad because he was concerned. So maybe Dad is trying to see if I'm okay. Maybe they've discussed how I screwed everything up with Eden, and maybe they both think that, being older and wiser, they could give me advice to fix it. But neither of them says anything, so maybe Sam kept his mouth shut after all.

We're on Main Street now. I've had this tour before, more times than I can remember. When I was little, I loved it. We have pictures of us standing outside my dad's high school, or at the playground where he learned to swing, climbing up the slide he spent his childhood sliding down.

Sam is taking the tour seriously. You can tell he wishes he could take notes, or that he had a way to record my father's narrative. Maybe Sam's a journalist—I never asked my dad what he did for a living.

"Hey, Sam," I call up to the front seat. I have to repeat it again, louder, to get a response. "Sam!"

He twists his neck around to see me. "Yeah?"

"What do you do?"

"For a living?"

"Yeah."

"I'm a doctor," he says, and turns back around, like no further explanation is needed. Not what kind of doctor he is, or whether he works at a hospital or has a private practice. I lean against the window, the glass cool on my forehead, and I close my eyes and imagine that right now Eden is sitting on her bed, reading the new biography of Teddy Roosevelt—no, Marie Antoinette—that she probably just picked up at the bookstore. The book is big and heavy in her hands, so she shifts on the bed, sitting up now with the book on her lap. She bites the nail on her right thumb, her lips just grazing the freckle below her cuticle. When her hair falls into her face, she pushes it back. Maybe she even knows that I'm watching her, just like she knew the difference between a boy who really didn't love her and a boy whose emotions were so ragged he couldn't pick out which of the things he was feeling was what he felt for her.

"We're here," my dad says triumphantly from the front seat.

The car has stopped. Dad and Sam are pulling on their coats, opening their doors. I didn't realize this was going to be a park-and-walk kind of tour.

I've been here plenty of times before; it's the land where my dad's grandparents had their farm. Dad's parked in the driveway of their old house. My dad and his parents lived there until he was three.

"Brandt Farm," my dad says proudly, stepping up the path

toward the house. Sam and I follow behind him. The wet ground feels heavy under my boots. I feel like I'm on a tour at a national park or something.

Dad goes to open the door.

"Dad," I call to his back—Sam and I are walking much more slowly—"You can't just go in."

"Why not? No one lives here."

"Yeah, but it's not your house."

"Sure it is."

I shrug. I guess he feels like since his family owned it, since he lived here once, since he still calls the land Brandt Farm, it still belongs to him.

The inside of the house feels like it has nothing to do with anything going on outside; it just smells wet and empty. You can't tell it's Christmastime; you can't even tell it's wintertime. Even though it's obviously uninhabited, I feel like we're trespassing.

Dad's giving a tour. "That was my parents' room. My crib was right there."

"How can you remember where your crib was?" I ask.

"I just do."

Sam's being quiet. He doesn't seem uncomfortable inside the house.

"The land's actually still good for farming," Dad continues. "But of course, there's no one to farm it."

"What do you know about whether land is good for farming?" I ask.

Dad shrugs, smiling. "Not a thing, I guess."

"Well, then how do you know?"

"That's what they told me when I bought the land."

"You bought this land?"

He nods. "Of course."

"What do you mean, of course?"

"My parents couldn't afford to keep it anymore."

"So, you bought it?"

"Sure."

"What for?" I ask. Sam is still quiet, staying close to the walls while my father and I stand in the middle of what used to be my grandparents' bedroom.

"I didn't want to lose it."

"But why?"

"Your grandfather grew up here, and his father before him, and his before him. It's Brandt Farm. My family has owned this land for so long that the street outside is named after us." I knew that: Brandt Way.

"But no one lives here; they could have sold it to someone who could use it."

"I can use it."

"Is this your way of telling me that you're uprooting us to Ohio?"

Dad smiles. I think he appreciates that I'm making a joke.

"It's important to keep a piece of where you came from," he says. "A big piece is better, if you can find one."

I don't say anything, but I look at Sam. I wonder if he feels connected to this farm any more than I do. My name may be all over it, but Sam is the one who was born in Troy, and both of his birth parents grew up here. By the time I was born, my father had been in New York, married to a New Yorker, for years.

"Let's take a walk out back," Dad says, holding his arm out to Sam, gesturing toward the back door. And it seems that there is so much about my dad I never knew before. I never knew how important Ohio was to him; I always assumed he'd felt lucky to get out, to have made it to New York. The life in which he had this other son seems intricately connected to this life where he bought emotionally significant real estate. And that life really isn't separate from the one he leads with us in New York.

It's stopped raining, and Sam and I fall in step next to each other across the backyard. My dad walks ahead of us again, up the hill behind the house; I know where he's headed.

"Sam," I whisper, "this is his favorite part."

"Huh?" Sam says blankly.

"He never gets tired of this joke."

"What joke?"

"He thinks it's funny to show people the outhouse."

Sam stops walking; so do I. And then he starts laughing, so much that I laugh, too.

"Your dad has a strange sense of humor."

"Yeah, I know," I say, and I look up at my dad. He must've stopped when he heard us laughing, because he's looking down at us now. And he's smiling so softly that I think he's actually going to start to glow.

When we're finally back in the car and pulling out of the driveway, my dad rolls down his window, takes a breath, and says, "Smell that?" I think he's making another outhouse joke, but he continues, "It still smells like my grandmother here. Isn't that something?"

We drive in silence for a little while, and as we pull off the highway toward the Days Inn, he says quietly, "You see, I know my parents won't be here forever. I just want there to always be something that connects me to this place."

And I know he means more than the place where he grew up, more than the place where Brandts have owned land for generations. He also means the place where Sam was born. And Sam must know it, too, because he rests his hand on my dad's shoulder, just for a second, after Dad says it.

The Lone Star State

All four of us—Dad, Mom, Sam, and I—drive Sam to the airport. I think my dad didn't want to be alone after Sam left. I guess it's possible that this will be the last time they ever see each other. Like maybe, having found his biological father and seen his biological town, Sam might be done with us now. Maybe, but I don't think it's likely.

"Do you have your ticket and your ID?" Dad asks Sam. The four of us are standing just outside of security, saying good-bye.

"Dad," I say before Sam can answer, "they're in his hand."

My dad looks down at Sam's hands. "Oh. I didn't realize."

"No worries, Rob," Sam says. They both look and sound more nervous than they did when Sam walked into my grandparents' house yesterday.

Dad's staring at Sam's hands now; he reaches for the empty one and holds it up next to his, and smiles.

He lets Sam's hand go and says, " 'Cause they hate when you slow the line down looking for your ticket and your ID."

"I know, Rob," Sam answers, smiling.

"Well, anyway."

"Anyway," Sam echoes.

"Well, Sam. I really hope—I hope that you got what you—that is, I tried to show you—I mean that it was really something—"

Mercifully, Sam interrupts, "It was wonderful, just wonderful, to meet you and your family, Rob."

Dad smiles and looks Sam straight in the eyes. "It was very nice meeting you, too, Sam." I can see he's tearing up, and I take a step closer; I don't know why—do I think my dad is going to fall or something? But he surprises me by putting his arm around me—one around me, and one around Sam.

He takes a deep breath. "Yes, it was very nice. . . . Nick," he says suddenly, turning and looking at me, "why does your jacket smell like cigarette smoke?"

I don't say anything. I look at Sam; I'm trying not to laugh. But Sam keeps his cool.

"That's my fault, Rob," he says, a sorry tone in his voice. "I smoked in our room last night."

My dad turns to face Sam now. "But, Sam, you're a doctor." He sounds disappointed, just as though he were scolding me. But I'm not jealous, because Sam looks over my father's head, to me, and he smiles. This is something just between us.

Sam looks back at my dad. "Don't worry, Rob, I'm quitting," he promises.

"Well, good," Dad answers, and over his head I grin at Sam. Stevie will like this story, I think; Stevie will like Sam.

My parents and I don't leave right away. We watch Sam head toward the security line, and I realize there is something I need to ask him before he goes.

"Wait one sec," I say to my parents, and I trot away from them.

"Hey, Sam," I call, and he turns around.

"How'd you make it right?" I ask.

"How'd I make what right?"

"In high school, when you broke up with Catherine, when you told her your love was a joke. How'd you get her back, after saying something so awful?"

Sam smiles at me. "I called her house a lot, woke up her parents at all hours. I did it so many times that I had to find new ways to say I'm sorry."

"That's all—you called her?"

"Well, it wasn't easy—I called until my fingers could punch in her number without looking, like I was reading Braille. And I had to throw in the occasional grand gesture—but yeah, it worked. I told you, Nick, she was smarter than I was." He grins. "Still is."

And as I walk back to my waiting parents, I know that this is definitely not the last we'll see of Sam.

And I don't mind. I'm actually kind of happy about it.

Phone Calls and Other Life-Altering Events

W e don't talk on the ride back to the Days Inn. It's raining and I lean my forehead against the window, even though the glass is wet and cold. It actually feels very calm in the car with my parents, like we're all kind of relieved that's over with. Not because it was so bad, but because Sam isn't some idea anymore. He's just a man, with flaws like cigarette smoke, walking down the Jetway now, making his way home.

I thought my father would be sad to see him go, but he's smiling. My mom is smiling, too, and maybe so am I. Maybe there is a different kind of love that I didn't know about before: I knew about the filial kind that comes out of being a family; the romantic kind that you fall into; the kind that you have with your best friend that you would never admit to out loud. But there is also something else, something that my dad felt for thirty years, some kind of connection that must come when you've had a child, even if you never knew him. Maybe my father felt some kind of chemical-reaction-type love so that he needed to meet Sam, needed to know that he was okay. Maybe I felt it, too, some blood-pull that made me need to know who Sam was. And now that we do, maybe there will be some other, some more peaceful kind of feeling to take its place.

I can feel my phone vibrating against my leg, tucked away in the pocket of my jeans. I know it's Stevie calling, to find out why I haven't called for over twenty-four hours. But I couldn't very well have called Stevie last night to let him know that I wouldn't be calling him because I was sharing a room with Sam. And I don't think I can pick up the phone now, either, since it feels like I'm not supposed to break the warm silence that fills the car.

It all began, when you think about it, with a ringing phone. Sam calling during *Wheel of Fortune;* me picking up, thinking it was a telemarketer. And it all started when I called Eden, inviting myself to her house to study, imagining what her bedroom looked like, picturing how white her stomach would be when she stretched her arms over her head.

At the motel, my parents head for their room, and I head for mine. The sofa where Sam slept is still made up like a bed, and I sit on the edge of it. It feels strange to sit on someone else's bed;

it feels strange to have the room all to myself; one night, and I'd gotten used to sharing it. But now I have the privacy I need to make the call I'm about to make.

I pull my phone out of my pocket and rest it on the bed beside me. I get up; take off my coat, my jeans, and my sweater; go into the bathroom and brush my teeth, splash some water on my face. I'm getting ready for the call like I'm getting ready for bed. 'Cause I know that this may take a while.

The screen on my phone says four missed calls, all from Stevie. This would be easier if at least one of them were from her, but it's not like I've given her any reason to call me lately.

I dial the number, deliberately not picking it from speed-dial. I like the feeling of knowing the number by heart, like the sound of the buttons clicking under my fingers. When the phone rings, once, twice, I think of Sam.

I wonder what Sam must have been thinking, that first time he called our house, hearing the phone ring—and I remember that I let it ring a good four or five times before I finally picked up. He must have been wondering what the voice on the other end was going to sound like. Would the right person pick up? Would his voice be gruff, deep, warm? Maybe he'd have an accent. Or maybe this wouldn't be the right number after all; maybe he moved, or the adoption registry might have gotten it wrong, or Sam might have written the number down incorrectly. Or maybe no one would pick up. Or maybe, worst of all, the person on the other end wouldn't want to talk at all.

That's what I'm scared of, as I listen to the phone ring, as I imagine Eden getting up from her bed to pick the phone up

from her desk, looking down and seeing that it's me who's calling. She might not want to talk to me. But I know I'll keep calling until she does. I'll make this right. Because she was right, just
like Sam's fiancée was right: We're the lucky kind.

It all begins with a ringing phone.

There is no one *thing that's true. It's all true.*
—*Ernest Hemingway,*
For Whom the Bell Tolls

Many, many thanks to my friends, family, and teachers at Random House Children's Books, at the Gernert Company, and at home.

I am I because my little dog knows me.
—Gertrude Stein

In Memoriam
Sara Jane Gravitt